Glamour

Glamour

On the Runway

Melody Carlson

BOOK FIVE

ZONDERVAN®

ZONDERVAN.com/
AUTHORTRACKER
follow your favorite authors

ZONDERVAN

Glamour
Copyright © 2011 by Melody Carlson

This title is also available as a Zondervan ebook.
Visit www.zondervan.com/ebooks.

Requests for information should be addressed to:

Zondervan, *Grand Rapids, Michigan 49530*

Library of Congress Cataloging-in-Publication Data

Carlson, Melody.
Glamour / Melody Carlson.
    p. cm. — (On the runway ; bk. 5)
    ISBN 978-0-310-71790-4 (softcover)
    [1. Reality television programs—Fiction. 2. Television—Production and
direction—Fiction. 3. Fashion—Fiction. 4. Sisters—Fiction. 5. Interpersonal
relations—Fiction. 6. Christian life—Fiction.] I. Title.
PZ7.C216637Glc 2011
[Fic]—dc22   2010037263

Cover design: Connie Gabbert, Faceout Studios
Interior design and composition: Patrice Sheridan, Tina Henderson,
Greg Johnson/Textbook Perfect

Printed in the United States of America

11 12 13 14 15 /DCI/ 21 20 19 18 17 16 15 14 13 12 11 10 9 8 7 6 5 4 3 2

Glamour

Chapter

1

After nearly six months of drama and chaos connected to *Malibu Beach*, I hoped we'd finally left the show behind. Far behind. And really, it seemed a natural assumption. Especially after Paige permanently distanced herself from Benjamin Kross, who'd already left the reality show, by getting engaged to the brilliant young designer Dylan Marceau last month in London. Apparently I was wrong. Because now, when Paige and I would rather be focusing on the Bahamas' beaches (since that's our next big trip), we are talking about Malibu Beach. Again.

It turns out that *Malibu Beach* is the reality show that keeps on giving. Its producers want to give us the "opportunity" to devote an entire *On the Runway* episode to one of their stars. Brogan Braxton, who has never liked Paige or me, recently declared herself a fashion expert. And now she's coming out with a new line of clothing called The BBB, which stands for Brogan Braxton Beachwear.

"But these are awful," Paige tells Helen Hudson as we all lean forward to peer at the images on the screen of Fran's laptop computer.

"I have to admit I'm with my sister on this one," I tell them. "What made Brogan Braxton suddenly decide she's a designer?"

"You mean besides Daddy's wallet?" Paige teases.

"I think you're missing the point," Fran says as she closes the laptop.

Helen adjusts her glasses and clears her throat. "Brogan Braxton is still one of the hottest commodities in the teen market."

Fran waves a piece of paper. "According to this, Brogan has almost as many Facebook friends as Ellen DeGeneres."

"Yes, and they're *real* friends too." I roll my eyes. I may be the last person on this continent to join Facebook, but I'm still holding out.

"I consider my Facebook friends to be real," Paige says to me in a slightly wounded way.

"Yes, and I'm sure they'd still be your friends if you didn't have a show, right?" I turn back to Helen. She's encouraging me to take a bigger role in our show, and I am trying. "But I thought we were talking about fashion, and I still don't get how Brogan Braxton, or The BBB … which, by the way, also stands for the Better Business Bureau, and I wonder how they feel about—"

"You're still missing the point," Fran says with a bit of aggravation.

"Remember the *R* word, girls?" Helen asks in a slightly bored tone.

"Ratings." Paige sighs. "Never mind whether it's fashionable or not, as long as the viewers tune in."

"Wait a minute," I say. "Just because we feature a fashion designer doesn't mean we have to approve of her style, does it?"

"That's true." Paige nods. "And my fans expect me to be honest. Do you have a problem if we do the show and I express my candid opinions about The BBB?"

Helen shrugs then pushes her chair away from the conference table. "Just keep the fans happy, Paige. Keep the ratings up." She stands and peers down at my sister. "And keep it clean."

"Oh, you know I always keep it clean, Helen." Paige flashes a camera-ready smile.

Helen pats Paige's cheek. "Yes, darling, but you know what I mean. Keep it polite and respectable. You have an image to maintain. One element that makes *On the Runway* different from other reality shows is that Paige Forrester, for the most part, is a lady. And the sponsors seem to appreciate that."

"You don't ask for much," Fran says to Helen. "Just keep the ratings up and play nice. That's so easy to do."

"Yes, well, our Paige is quite expert at it." Helen laughs as she heads for the door. "Sorry to meet and run, girls, but I have a major appointment with the network in about ten minutes. Ta-ta!"

Fran shuffles some papers into a stack then slides them over to her assistant, Leah. "Brogan's show is scheduled for this Saturday at two." Fran gets a worried look. "That's not your mom's wedding date, is it?"

"No, that's the following weekend," Paige says. "You are coming, aren't you?"

"Yes, of course, I already RSVP'd. I just blanked it." Fran takes a long drink from her bottle of water.

"The crew is scheduled already," Leah fills in for her. "You girls can come to wardrobe around ten, then we'll head over to the site and do the pre-show shoot. After the fashion show, we'll do the wrap-up." She smiles. "The usual stuff."

I'm curious as to why Leah is briefing us, since that's what Fran usually does. But maybe Leah is also trying to take a more active role.

"Brogan wants to do an interview before the runway show," Fran begins then looks at Leah. "When is that scheduled?"

"She asked for Wednesday afternoon," Leah tells us. "Two o'clock … on *Malibu Beach* turf."

Paige frowns. "So Brogan called and asked us to interview her?"

"Her people called us," Leah clarifies.

"We thought we might get something to use for the show," Fran says.

"The interview is just with Brogan?" Paige asks. "Not any other cast members or the *Malibu Beach* crew, right?"

"I'm not sure about that," Fran tells her. "In fact, it sounds as if their crew will be filming this too. Just in case it's show-worthy."

"You mean in case they want to *make* it show-worthy." Paige groans. "Something about this whole thing is starting to smell fishy. It's no secret that Brogan doesn't exactly like me. This is not some kind of setup, is it—*a get Paige plot?*"

"No, of course not." Fran shakes her head.

"Because I know Brogan was pretty close to Mia Renwick. I mean, they weren't *best* friends. When Mia died, though, it was like everyone in the cast suddenly decided they had been her very best friends. I can understand that. But I also understand that some of those girls seriously hate me, Fran. Including Brogan."

"At least you're not with Ben now," I remind her.

"I hear he's getting back with Waverly Stratton," Leah says in a gossipy tone. "I saw it on *WWW* last weekend."

"The World Wide Web?" I ask.

Leah laughs. "No, that new entertainment show, *Who's Who and Why*. Haven't you seen it?"

I shake my head, thinking maybe it should be called *Who's Who and Who Cares?*

"Really, Erin," she tells me, "you need to keep up. Anyway, they showed some pics of Waverly and Benjamin at a club, and in the interview Waverly said they were together."

Paige looks skeptical. "That was a stretch on Waverly's part."

"So back to the topic at hand." Fran taps her pen impatiently. "What exactly are you saying, Paige? That you don't want to work with Brogan?"

"I just don't want to be sabotaged and end up on their show looking like an evil, backstabbing witch like that other time."

"Seriously, Paige, what could they actually do?" I ask her. "If it starts to go sideways, we'll just walk out." I turn to Fran. "Right?"

She nods and takes another sip of water.

"Speaking of walking out"—Leah holds up her Black-Berry—"don't you need to get moving, Paige? I have you scheduled for that spot on *ET* this afternoon, remember?"

Paige stands suddenly. "That's right."

"Why don't you let me drive you?" Leah offers. "That way you can get ready on the way over there. And you'll be on time."

"Great idea." Paige reaches into her bag then tosses me her car keys. "Guess I'll see you at home." And just like that, they're gone.

I turn to Fran and study her for a moment.

"*What?*" she says.

"Are you ... *okay?*" I use what I hope is a gentle voice.

She shrugs and reaches for her bag. "I'm fine." We both get up, but before we leave the conference room, I decide to try again.

"Really, Fran, you don't seem like yourself. Is something bothering you?"

And then, like I pressed the wrong button or something, she starts to crumble. Tears are coming and her hands are shaking, which makes me wonder if I should've kept my big mouth closed. I go over and close the blinds on the glass door and ask her to sit back down. "What's wrong?" I ask.

"I didn't want anyone to know—to know—that—" She chokes in a sob.

"Know *what?*" I'm seriously worried now. Something is really wrong.

She looks at me with watery eyes. "My cancer is back."

I blink. "You had cancer?"

"Had ... and now I have it again."

I put my hand on her arm. "Oh, Fran."

"I was diagnosed with leukemia in my early thirties. I went through all the treatments and they seemed to have worked. I thought it was gone. And now I have it again."

"I'm so sorry."

She nods as she opens her bag and retrieves a packet of tissues, pulls one out, then wipes her eyes. "I've been in remission for almost six years. Six years!" She blows her nose. "And five years is considered cured. I really believed I was cured."

"But you're getting treatment?"

"I started chemo last Friday."

"Does Helen know?"

Fran shakes her head. "No one knows. Today I told Leah I was feeling under the weather and asked if she would help me out in the meeting."

"I wondered why she was more involved."

"But I don't know if I can hide it for the whole time ... I mean while I'm doing chemo."

I don't know what to say. I've never known anyone with cancer before.

"Promise me you won't tell anyone," she begs. "I wouldn't have told you, Erin, except you pushed me. And I trust you. Just promise you won't tell."

I nod. "Sure. It's not my place to talk about your personal life to anyone."

"I want to be realistic, and if I can't do my job ... well, I will deal with that when the time comes." She forces a smile. "But my oncologist is quite positive. She says the new drugs are better than before. She really thinks the chemo will wipe it out again."

"But doesn't chemo kind of wipe a person out too?" I ask. "I mean, how can you expect to work while you're going through treatment?" I don't point out that, even today, she seemed wasted ... and she's barely begun her chemo.

"My doctor seems to think it's a possibility. A lot of people continue with their jobs during treatment. There are some new anti-nausea meds that are supposed to be really effective. I just have to take it easy, get lots of rest, drink water, and eat the right foods."

"Oh ..." I'm trying to absorb this, but it just doesn't make sense. I always assumed that if a person had cancer, they needed time off to get treatment and recover.

"I *have* to work, Erin." Her eyes look desperate. "Not just financially, because I know insurance will help. My work is my life. Without it, I wouldn't have a chance of surviving this. Can you understand that?"

"I guess so." Although I silently question how or why work should be anyone's life. "But, as your friend, I want you to do whatever it takes to get well. That's the important thing. Can you understand *that*?"

Fran smiles. "You're such a good kid, Erin."

I shrug. "Yeah, well . . ."

"Not that you're such a kid. You're mature for your age, and you have a really good head on your shoulders. I know I can trust you with this."

"Of course."

"I want to go to Bahamas Fashion Week with you girls. I've really been looking forward to it. I don't know what I'd do if I missed out on that . . ." She looks close to tears again. "It would feel like . . . like the cancer had won."

I take in a slow breath. "Then you have to do everything you can to get well." I think about the timeline. "But that gives you less than four weeks. Can you be healthy enough to travel by then?"

"That's my goal."

"And you won't go if your doctor recommends against it?"

She pauses as if considering. "No, of course not. That would be foolish."

"If there's anything I can do to help," I offer, "please, feel free to ask. I mean that, Fran. I wouldn't say it if I didn't mean it."

"Thanks, Erin. I believe you. I'll keep that in mind." She flashes a funny grin. "So, how are you at holding a girlfriend's hair back while she worships at the porcelain throne?"

"Huh?"

She chuckles. "You never were a party girl, were you?"

"Not so much."

She pats my shoulder. "One of the things I admire about you. You are *so you*." She slowly stands. "I think I need to get home now ... I need to get some rest."

We walk out to the parking lot together and, although Fran is quiet, my brain is buzzing like a caffeinated mosquito. Whether it makes sense or not, I am suddenly feeling very responsible. Not only for Fran's well-being, but for how it might impact our show if she's trying to direct us when she really should be home in bed. It's got me very worried, and I think Helen should be informed. And yet I know I have to keep my promise to Fran.

"You take care now," I say as I wait for her to get into her car. "Promise you'll call me if you need anything."

She gives me a weak smile as she puts her window down. "Yeah. And you promise not to worry about me. Okay?"

I nod, knowing that's a promise I might not be able to keep.

"Leah will call with the details on the interview with Brogan. I'll see you on Wednesday."

"Get some rest," I say as her window goes up. She makes another weak smile, then drives away. Suddenly I feel like crying. *Poor Fran!* Why is this happening to her? But instead of breaking down in the parking lot, I slowly walk over to Paige's car, and as I walk, I pray. I ask God to do a miracle in Fran's life. I'm not exactly sure what kind of a miracle I have in mind, although I'm trusting that God knows what's best. But that's what I'm expecting—a real honest-to-goodness miracle.

Chapter 2

"Is there a better form of torture than this?"
Mollie drapes a little black-lace camisole over her huge, pregnant belly with a frown.

I have to control myself from laughing at the image. "I'm sorry," I tell her, "but you're the one who wanted to come to Victoria's Secret tonight."

Mollie puts the camisole back. "Why did Paige insist on having a personal shower for your mom anyway?"

"Because she's seen my mom's lingerie wardrobe, which is a stretch in terms, and it's so sad that even my conservative underwear looks good in comparison." I pull out a red-and-black silk kimono and hold it up.

"Can't be any worse than the maternity undies I'm wearing these days."

"Well, maybe after your baby comes, you can go underwear shopping for yourself." I put the kimono back. "And like I told you," I remind her, "you can just get her some shower gel or something like that."

"No." Mollie stubbornly shakes her head. "Your mom has been like a second mom to me and I want to get her something really special." She holds up a short, coral-colored satin robe. "How about this?"

I nod. "That actually looks like something she'd like. And that color would be good on her too."

"Done." Mollie heads for the cashier. It's strange seeing my best friend so pregnant. She still has almost two months until her due date, but she's gotten so huge that, thanks to her lack of height, she's starting to look almost as wide as she is tall. Not that I'd ever say that to her, or anything else that might upset her. Mollie's been extremely moody lately. I'm sure it has to do with hormones, but sometimes I feel like I'm walking on eggshells with her.

"Now that that's done, I'm starving," she announces as we're leaving the store. "I'm craving ice cream. With hot fudge, I think."

I know better than to question this or to suggest something healthier. "I guess so," I tell her.

"I'll treat," she offers. "My thank you for you bringing me here, especially after you already got your shower present."

I'm a little concerned about Mollie's expenditures tonight. Usually she's pretty frugal, and that robe was not cheap. But, again, I know better than to mention this. And, really, it's none of my business.

"So are you guys going to do the interview with Brogan Braxton tomorrow?" she asks after we're seated with our sundaes. I really didn't want a whole sundae, but Mollie wouldn't take no for an answer.

"I think so." I dip my spoon and swirl it around.

"Is Paige okay with it?"

"Cautiously okay," I admit. "We devised a cue system in case we want to cut it short."

"What is it?" She licks the chocolate from her spoon.

"Paige will say *polka-dot bikini* to tip me off."

"How do you use *polka-dot bikini* in a normal conversation?"

I shrug. "Paige will manage. Besides, Brogan's line is beachwear."

"Beachwear." Mollie dips her spoon again. "There's something I don't need to worry about this summer. Unless someone has a beached whale beachwear line."

"You're not going to be this big forever, Moll."

"That's what they say." She looks down at her enormous midsection. "I'm just finding it hard to believe."

"August isn't that far off either," I point out.

"That reminds me," she says a bit more brightly. "My obstetrician thinks my due date might be off."

"Off?"

"Yeah. At the last ultrasound, she said it looks like the baby is more developed, like maybe I was off. She said it could be more like mid-July."

"Hey, that's great. The baby will be here even sooner."

"Yeah, but now I'm worried you won't be back from the Bahamas when it comes."

"Oh … yeah." Mollie has coerced me into being her birthing coach. "Do you still want me to go to the childbirth classes with you?"

"Yeah, but maybe I'll reschedule for the end of June. Is that okay?"

"Sure." I don't want to make her feel bad, but I know I need to ask. "Do you have a backup plan? I mean, if I'm still in the Bahamas when you go into labor?"

"My mom will help."

"Oh, good." I try not to look too relieved. "So, she's coming around more?" I don't want to say too much, because Mollie's mom has been kind of up and down in regard to this baby. Some days she's happy she'll be a grandma. Other times, especially if she's been talking to Mollie's dad too much, she can be extremely negative. Mollie's dad has made no secret that he wants Mollie to give the baby up for adoption. But Mollie seems firm in her choice to keep and raise her child.

"Yeah, Mom's been pretty cool lately. She's so certain it's going to be a girl that she's even bought some clothes."

"And you're sticking with your resolve ... not to find out the sex of the baby until it arrives."

Mollie nods as she dips her spoon into the ice cream.

"Well, I hope that I'm here for you when the time comes."

"Me too." She frowns and pushes her half-eaten ice cream away. "Now I'm stuffed."

As I drive Mollie home, I think, not for the first time, that it's not easy being a best friend to an unmarried pregnant girl. For one thing, I can't speak my mind openly ... not like I used to anyway. I want to ask Mollie if she's heard from Tony lately, or whether he ever plans to step up and accept some responsibility for this child. But I know that usually just upsets her. I also want to ask if he's quit pressuring her to give the baby up for adoption. Last I heard, he was getting legal advice. I think he needs mental advice. Of course, I also want to ask if she has given her decision enough thought. But I know where that will get us — and I just don't want to go there.

Still, after I drop her at home, I try to imagine what her life's going to be like with a baby, not in her tummy, but in her arms. A baby that wants to be fed and burped and changed and cared for 24/7. Has she really taken this into consideration? I also wonder how that's going to affect our friendship.

I know it's selfish of me to think this, but I'm not sure I want to be hanging with Mollie and her baby all the time. And that makes me feel seriously guilty.

It also makes me feel like I need another best friend. Not to replace Mollie, because I think we will always be best friends, but just someone to fill in the gap when she's busy being a mommy. I wonder if it's wrong to feel that way.

As I go up to the condo, I'm thinking of Blake. He's kind of like an alternative best friend, but for some reason he's been a little out of touch lately. In fact, I think it's time to give my old buddy a call. But when I try, I get his voicemail and so I leave a message.

"Hey, Blake. I'm missing you. What's up? Maybe this is dead week. Or maybe you're having finals. If so, good luck. Call me when you're not busy." As I hang up, I realize I probably nailed it. This is the first week of June, so he's probably ending the school year. But as I get ready for bed, I'm questioning this. Even if it's dead week or if he's having finals, he could call me. And now I wonder if he might be avoiding me for some other reason. I wonder if I offended him the last time we talked, when we went to see a movie.

So as I get into bed, I replay our last conversation. It took place more than a week ago and it had to do with our relationship.

"So, now that Paige is engaged," he had begun, "I assume your agreement with her—to lay off dating relationships—is kind of moot?"

I told him that Paige could make her own decisions, but I still felt like I wasn't ready for a serious relationship.

"Define a serious relationship," he challenged me.

"You know, steady, committed, exclusive."

He had just nodded, but now that I think about it, it seems like his eyes were troubled. Or maybe I'm imagining it.

"Don't you agree with that?" I asked him.

"I guess so."

"So we're on the same page then?"

"Sure. If you don't want our relationship to be steady, committed, or exclusive, how can I not agree?"

"But you really are my best guy friend," I assured him. "And I'm thankful for you."

As I recall, he had smiled. We held hands as we went into the theater, and everything seemed pretty much the same as it's been for the past few months. But maybe something changed that night. When I consider his goodnight kiss, I feel even more certain of this.

"You're a great girl," he told me that night. "And you've been a good friend to me."

"Same back at you," I said to him.

Then we had kissed. And when he stopped kissing me, he had this sad expression. "See you around, Erin."

At the time I remember thinking it was a weird way to say goodnight. Then I got busy with life and work and helping get things ready for Mom's upcoming wedding, and I didn't think too hard about it. Until now.

It's possible I could be over-thinking this, like Paige is always accusing me of doing. And lately, it seems there is plenty to think about. So, as I open my Bible, my regular bedtime routine, I tell myself that everything between Blake and me is just fine. Same old, same old. I'm guessing that by the end of the week, Blake will call. If he doesn't, I'll call him and invite him to the BBB fashion show. Knowing Blake, that's an invite he will not refuse.

On Wednesday morning, Paige and I go to the studio, where Paige spends about an hour in wardrobe, putting together our outfits.

"I want us to look impeccable," she tells me as she holds the white Michael Kors jacket in front of me, studying me and it carefully as if she's about to change her mind again.

She has just decided to stick with Michael Kors for me when Fran and Leah arrive. Although I try not to stare, I can't help noticing how weak and pale Fran looks. Paige shows her selections to Fran, and naturally Fran approves. Who would dare disapprove Paige's fashion sense? Certainly not anyone who's not feeling her best.

"Let's get you girls started in hair and makeup," Fran tells us. "We'll go over some of the show details on the way there." She gives Leah instructions and says she'll be in her office. Hopefully not throwing up.

"What's troubling you?" Shauna asks as I sit in the chair for makeup.

"Nothing."

She reaches for a sponge. "Well, for a moment you looked like you lost your best friend."

I force a smile.

"See." She points to the mirror. "You know what they say about a smile? It increases your face value."

"Yeah, I think you've told me that one before, Shauna."

"Apparently it didn't take then either." She chuckles. "Now close your eyes." As she works, she rattles on about how a positive attitude is life changing. "It's like an internal makeover," she says as she applies eyeliner.

"I agree," I mumble. I know she doesn't like us to talk much while she's working on our faces. "Thanks for the reminder."

After a bit, Paige and I switch chairs, and by twelve thirty we're ready to get dressed, but Leah has brought in some lunch, and so we all sit around and eat and talk instead.

"I told the camera guys about the polka-dot bikini line," Leah informs Paige. "Hopefully, you won't need to use it."

"Hopefully." Paige forks a piece of pineapple.

By one fifteen we're dressed and on our way to the studio where the interview will be shot. Leah informs us it's a studio Brogan picked.

"We did suggest a neutral location," Fran tells us.

"But Brogan insisted this was better," Leah says.

"Naturally, the studio is owned by the same network that produces *Malibu Beach*." Fran leans back in the seat and sighs. I wonder how she's feeling, but don't dare ask.

Paige wrinkles her nose as we get out of the car. "It feels like we're going into enemy territory."

As we enter the studio, it's reassuring to see our camera guys already there and set up. As is the *Malibu Beach* crew. Unfortunately, there are a few other members of the *Malibu Beach* cast there as well. They're keeping a low profile around the sidelines, but even so, it's starting to feel a little like high noon at the O.K. Corral.

"Ready for this?" I quietly ask Paige.

She nods with a perfect smile. "I am a professional."

"And don't forget it," Fran tells her as she finds a chair and sits.

Leah does some last-minute touches to Paige's hair and then we're mic'd up. We're told to head onto the platform that's arranged with three chairs and some potted palms in back. I check to make sure I have my note cards in my pocket. I know my role is to be supportive of Paige and to jump in as needed, but I feel nervous as we greet Brogan, making small talk like we're all old friends.

I try to act natural, but I'm still getting used to my new role in the limelight. I say a silent prayer as we're seated and final adjustments are made to mic cords, sound, and lights.

"I want to keep this casual," Paige tells Brogan.

"Great." Brogan keeps a stiff smile on her face.

Our camera guy, Alistair, does the countdown and Paige speaks directly to the camera in her usual warm, friendly voice. "We're with Brogan Braxton today. As most of you know, Brogan is one of the stars of the reality TV show *Malibu Beach*. But what you may not know is that Brogan has some other tricks up her sleeves." She smiles at Brogan. "And those are some good-looking sleeves too."

"Thank you." Brogan sits a little straighter.

Paige looks back at the camera, explaining how Brogan is introducing her new line of beachwear. "We're here to find out more about this exciting new line of clothing." Paige turns to Brogan. "So, tell me, Brogan, what made you decide to design beachwear?"

"For starters, I've always loved fashion," Brogan begins, "but I've been disappointed by some of the designs we get to choose from."

"I know what you mean," Paige agrees. "When you're on the beach, or by the pool, you want to be stylish, but you also want to be comfortable. I remember a swimsuit I had that looked fantastic—unless I decided to move in it. Then the bottom would ride up, the top would slip down, and I'd end up looking like a case of indecent exposure." She laughs.

"Yes. My line, The BBB, isn't like that."

There's a brief pause, so I jump in. "Another thing about swimwear is that it's nice if you can actually *swim* in it."

Brogan looks surprised. "Well, yes, that is the point."

"So would you say your pieces hold up well in the water?" I persist. "Have they been pool tested? What about salt water? That can really mess up some suits."

Brogan looks stumped.

"That's an interesting question," Paige says to me. "I wonder how many swimwear designers actually do test their garments in the water. For instance, some fabrics hold their shape, but some get all loose and weird." She turns back to Brogan. "Did you take that into consideration with your line?"

"Well, I am working with some other designers."

"So the BBB line isn't exclusively your original designs?"

"Of course they're mine. It's my name on the label and nothing is made without my approval."

"Where did you train as a designer?" Paige frowns at her notes. "Actually, I see here that you haven't been to college yet. So I guess that means you don't have any official training."

"Well, no, I'm only nineteen."

"So, would you say you're naturally gifted at design?" Paige's smile looks a bit stiff.

"How about you?" Brogan tosses back at her. "You're the self-proclaimed fashion *expert*, right?"

Paige laughs uncomfortably. "I guess you could say that."

"You're not much older than I am." Brogan's eyes narrow. "And if you came here thinking you were going to humiliate me today—"

"Hey," Paige waves her hands toward the cameras. "We might as well cut if this is going to turn into a debate. That's not our purpose."

Naturally, the cameras are still rolling. After all, both crews know how reality shows operate. Fran steps in and invites us to take a break.

"Let's regroup," she suggests, her eyes tired.

Now I feel bad. Perhaps there was something I could've done to keep this on track. As we retreat to opposite sides of the studio, I ask myself what I need to do to help smooth this over.

Chapter 3

After about fifteen minutes, we all decide to try again. Paige makes some self-deprecating jokes about how she really has no formal training either, and how it's no big deal. "I guess we're both just naturally gifted," she tells Brogan. "We're just a couple of fashion freaks."

I know that's true for Paige, but I think it's an overstatement in regard to Brogan. I play along anyway. "I can attest to the fact that Paige has been studying fashion since she was little," I tell Brogan. "I remember the time she threw a spoiled-princess hissy fit because her shoes were the wrong shade of pink to go with her dress."

Brogan gives us a tolerant smile. "Yes, well, I suppose I'm a bit like that too." She sits straighter in her chair. "You see, I've always had a knack for fashion. My friends like to come to me for advice. And, like I said, I work with some good designers."

"So, I'm curious," Paige continues. "When it comes time to actually put the designs together, what kind of a role *do* you take?"

Brogan's eyes dart over to where her friends are watching. "I take a very active role. I'm very involved. I work closely with my designers. And I think when you see my show on Saturday, you'll understand why I'm so passionate about this."

I want to point out that we've already seen photos—unimpressive ones. But I know better.

"I think the design steps are so fascinating," Paige says with enthusiasm. "I just love every aspect of it. Don't you?"

"Absolutely." Brogan nods eagerly. "It's exciting to see how ideas become clothes."

"Perhaps we could visit you in your studio," I suggest to Brogan. "It would be fun to see you at work."

"Yes," Paige agrees. "In fact, that's how we usually interview designers."

"We might be able to arrange that." Brogan is getting cool again.

"I'm sure our viewers, and yours too, would love to see Brogan Braxton in her design mode."

Brogan nods but looks uncomfortable. And there's one of those pauses again.

"So do you draw the designs yourself?" I ask.

"Yes, of course."

"That's impressive," Paige tells her. "You must be something of an artist then."

Some of Brogan's friends giggle and Brogan frowns. "I mostly just do some initial pencil sketches."

"Do you actually sew some of the designs?" Paige asks.

Now there are more giggles, and Brogan scowls like that was a dumb question. "No. I have people who do that for me."

"It's just that I know a lot of designers who start out in a very hands-on sort of way," Paige explains. "Are you saying you're not involved in the initial construction of your garments? Not at all?"

"*Like I said, Paige,* I have people who do that for me. I'm more of an idea person."

"So you don't do any of the actual work?" I ask, trying to grasp what she's really saying—what exactly is it that makes Brogan Braxton a designer?

"My job is to *direct* my designers," Brogan explains. "I'm kind of like the queen bee with my worker bees buzzing about." She chuckles like she's enjoying her metaphor.

"I'm curious," I say. "How do you do that, exactly?"

"We meet regularly and discuss ideas and styles and lines," she says. "And, of course, I suggest colors."

"And you probably choose fabrics too?" Paige inserts.

"Yes. Absolutely." She nods. "I'm very hands-on when it comes to fabrics."

"Do you have a preference," Paige asks, "of, say, synthetic over natural fiber?"

"Oh, we use all kinds of fabrics." Brogan looks uncomfortable again. There's another pause, and I hope Paige uses our polka-dot bikini cue soon, as this is about the most boring interview my sister has ever conducted. It's not entirely Paige's fault; Brogan is about as interesting as a stump.

I decide to jump in again. "How concerned are you about how your clothing line impacts the environment?"

"Very concerned." She nods with big eyes.

"So what are you doing to keep your carbon footprint minimal? And do you use overseas laborers, and if so, do you practice fair—"

"I—uh—I have a guy who handles all that for me."

"So back to the design process," Paige says. "How do you

start thinking up a new line of swimwear? What inspires you, Brogan?"

As Brogan continues to ramble, it becomes increasingly clear that she knows very little about clothing and design. My guess is she's a puppet and it's her name, combined with her daddy's money, that drives The BBB.

Finally, the interview is over. The good news is that while there were some uncomfortable moments, there were no serious catfights. The bad news is that it was probably a total waste of time.

"Do we still have to cover the fashion show on Saturday?" I ask Paige as she and I are on our way home. "I mean, what's the point?"

"I plan to ask Helen about it," Paige tells me. "I have a bad feeling about the whole thing. And Helen cannot expect me to act like Brogan is some great designer. Seriously, she's clueless about design and she knows it."

"And your fans are going to know it," I tell Paige. "Even I can tell and I'm kind of clueless too."

Paige laughs. "I'd put your fashion sense up against Brogan's any day."

"Thanks ... I think."

All day Friday, Paige and I are obsessed with putting together the final details of Mom's bridal shower. More accurately, Paige is obsessed; I'm just trying to cooperate. And I'm trying to keep myself from saying, "Hey, it's just a shower." Paige seems determined to turn this event into the shower of the century. Or, more likely, she's just indoctrinating me for what she expects I'll do when her turn comes around. Although she and Dylan seem in no hurry to set a wedding date (thank goodness!), I can tell she's making plans and I've seen a stack of wedding magazines and notebooks in her room.

Anyway, we're having Mom's shower at her friend Jackie's, who has this really amazing house in Malibu. Jackie seems content to let Paige call the shots, which is smart since it's one of the things Paige does best. Well, that and bossing me around. It's like she thinks I'm her personal gopher. I go for this, I go for that. Eventually I go and pick up Mollie and hope that Paige's perfect evening is on track.

By the time my mom's friends are all gathered around and it's party time, I feel somewhat frazzled and worn out. Fortunately, Mom's friends are full of energy. I'm not sure if it's thanks to Jackie's margaritas, which she is handing out to those who are of age, or just something in the air, but this place is hopping. Paige, playing the role of happy hostess, is in her element, flitting around as the women visit loudly between the goofy games that Paige insists must be played. Even Mollie seems caught up in the merriment and she actually wins the last game, securing the prize of Godiva chocolates.

Eventually, with my ears still ringing from the noise, I retreat to the kitchen on the pretense of making sure that everything is going okay with the caterer. But just as I'm sneaking a delicious mini lobster cake, I hear what sounds like my cell phone ringing. When I track down my purse, which Paige must've shoved into the pantry along with hers, I see that it's Blake calling. I know, out of respect for my mom, that I should turn off my phone. But since I seriously doubt she will miss me, I answer.

"Hey, Blake," I say cheerfully as I head down a back hallway. "What's up?"

"I'm returning your call," he says in a voice that sounds strangely businesslike. "You left me a message."

"Yeah, like a week ago."

"I believe it was on Monday."

"Right." Now I'm feeling uncomfortable, almost as if I'd called him and caught him at a bad moment, but then I remember he's the one who called me.

"So did you have something to tell me?" he asks.

"No, not really ... I mean, I think I only called to say hi and to make sure you're doing okay. You are, aren't you? Okay, I mean?"

"Sure. I'm great. I just finished finals week." Now this sounds a bit more like the Blake I know—or thought I knew.

"I'll bet that feels good to be done with."

"Uh-huh."

I tell him about how we're having Mom's shower tonight and that I was just taking a little break from all the craziness.

"Which reminds me of something," he says in a formal voice.

"What's that?"

"Well, I kind of assumed we'd be together at your mom's wedding and all that ..."

"Yeah?" I'm getting a funny feeling.

"As you must know, that's not going to happen now and I didn't want to just leave it hanging. I know the wedding's next weekend and there's that dinner the night before and whatever. So I just figured I should talk to you, Erin. Just so we're on the *same page*."

As soon as he says "same page," I remember how I said those exact words to him last week. Somehow it feels like he's on a different page than I am now.

"You're not coming to my mom's wedding?"

"Oh, I'll still come if you want me to. I mean, I do have an invitation. Unless you'd like to uninvite me."

"No, of course not."

"And your mom is my friend too."

"Yes. Absolutely." I feel confused and slightly irritated.

"So I guess I'll still come then."

"Good." Now *my* voice sounds stiff and formal.

"Anyway, have a good shower. See you around."

"Thanks. See ya." As I hang up I shake my head. What's up with Blake? Why is he acting so weird? And was that what I thought it was—is he trying to dump me? Or did this actually happen last week? Maybe I dumped him and we're both just figuring it out now. And if that's what's going on, why does it feel so lousy?

I'm aware that we weren't in a serious, committed, or exclusive relationship. It's what I was trying to tell him last week. Even so, I thought we had *some* kind of a relationship. Good friends anyway. Very good friends. In fact, there've been times when I've felt closer to Blake than Mollie. But now what? It's just over? End of story?

I feel a lump in my throat as I go to the powder room, hoping to get a grip on my emotions. Really, this is ridiculous. Why should I feel like this, like someone just jerked the ground out from under me? Because I do. I feel blindsided ... and kind of betrayed too. I wonder if Blake did this to hurt me. If so, why? Why would he want to hurt me? Is that how friends treat each other?

Someone knocks on the door and I realize I need to move my pity party of one to another location.

"Erin!" gushes Abby, one of my mom's work friends. "This is such a great shower you girls planned for your mom."

"Thanks, it was mostly Paige's doing."

"Well, it's very fun."

Instead of going to where the women are still talking and laughing loudly, I slip out a back door and, with my phone still in my hand, sit on a deck chair and try to decide how to react. Should I call Blake back and demand to know what he means? I want to know what he's saying, what kind of a game he's playing, and whether or not he knows he hurt me. I almost push the speed dial and then I stop myself. What am I doing?

Seriously, what right do I have to question him? He's actually doing what I said I wanted. At least it's what I think I said I wanted . . . but is it what I *really* wanted? I'm not so sure about that. And if I did want it then, what if I don't want it now? But what if I do want it tomorrow?

Why am I so flaky?

After a few minutes of head-clearing, or what feels more like an emotional Ping-Pong game, I realize that I should get back to Mom's shower and at least give the appearance of being mentally present. Especially before Mollie comes looking for me and wants to know what's up. But as I rejoin the party, laughing and smiling, it feels like such an act. Underneath, I am miserable. Fortunately, no one seems to notice. Eventually the party winds down and I distract myself by cleaning up, until it's finally time to leave.

"Are you okay?" Mollie asks as I drive her home.

"Yeah, I'm fine." I attempt one of my party smiles, but I can tell it's wearing thin.

"You're sure?"

"Just tired," I tell her. "I'm so glad that shower is over with. Paige really pulled out all the stops, didn't she?"

"Your mom seemed to thoroughly enjoy it."

"Yeah . . ."

"Seriously, Erin, are you okay? You seem bummed about something. Are you worried about your mom's marriage? Jon seems like a great guy. Your mom seems really happy."

"No, that's not bothering me. I'm happy for both of them." I'm tempted to just spill my story. At the same time, I'm determined not to say anything about this to Mollie or anyone until I really know how I feel about everything. It's possible that I'm simply suffering hurt feelings, wounded pride, bruised self-esteem . . . all because Blake dumped me. Yet again.

Although, to be fair, you can't really dump someone if you're not in a serious relationship. So why am I taking this so hard? The truth is, I'm not even sure how I feel. What's the point of rehashing this whole thing, even with my best friend, until I figure out some things for myself? So, as I turn down Mollie's street, I explain that I'm tired and a little worried about tomorrow's fashion show, which is not untrue.

"Tell Paige not to let that snooty Brogan Braxton push her around," Mollie says as I pull up to her house.

"Why do you call her snooty?" My experiences with Brogan have been bad enough that I think she's snooty too, but Mollie has never actually met her.

"Don't you *ever* watch their show?"

I roll my eyes.

"Yeah, yeah, I know you think *Malibu Beach* is juvenile and a waste of time, but I can't help myself." She pats her big tummy. "It's not like I have a life. And, hey, you can make fun of me, but watching stupid kids doing stupid things makes me feel better about myself."

I can't help but laugh. "So it's kind of like therapy?"

She grins. "Yeah, and it's free too."

"So is Brogan pretty bad on the show?"

"She's a total brat." Mollie nods. "She's spoiled and selfish and—"

"Aren't those prerequisites for being on that show?"

"But Brogan is the worst of the lot. I'm not sure if it's because she's rich or what, but she treats her friends like dirt sometimes. Oh, not to their faces. She's manipulative and a hypocrite and a fake." Mollie opens the car door. "And her friends are starting to figure it out."

"But her friends were with her at the studio on Wednesday. Like they wanted to show support for her."

"Or else they're just looking for publicity ops."

"Maybe."

"Anyway, tell Paige to watch her back. You too."

I tell Mollie I'll do that and, as I drive home, my concern over Blake is overshadowed by my curiosity about how tomorrow's fashion show will go. It's been a while since Paige and I have had much to do with the *Malibu Beach* scene. Even Paige's involvement with Benjamin Kross, which thankfully is over, was kept separate from that show.

Wednesday was like a small sample of what we can expect and, for the most part, Paige seemed to be in control. Still, it was obvious that Brogan wasn't too thrilled with the interview. Not that she could blame us for her inept answers about being a "designer." Really, how did she think it was going to go down? I'm hoping we can make it through tomorrow's show without fireworks.

Chapter 4

I decide not to mention what Mollie said about Brogan Braxton as we're getting ready for the show. For one thing, I figure Paige already knows since she still (secretly) watches *Malibu Beach* sometimes. Plus, she's experienced Brogan's meanness firsthand. But, besides that, I'm hoping that maybe Brogan has grown up some. Even though she was a little difficult at Wednesday's interview, she wasn't exactly mean. Besides, this is her big day—why would she want to ruin it?

"Look how white you are," Paige says as we're leaving the studio with Fran.

I glance down at my bare arms and legs, which are rather pale, especially in the bright sunlight. We're wearing sundresses and sandals since today's fashion show will be outdoors and poolside at one of Hollywood's premiere hotels. "So?" I shrug. "At least I put on some sunscreen."

"But I told you to schedule a spray tan," Paige reminds me.

"I didn't have time," I tell her. "What with Mom's shower and all."

"How did that go?" Fran asks as we get into the car.

"That's right," Paige says, "you weren't there."

"Sorry to miss it." Fran makes an apologetic smile. "I had a migraine."

"Are you feeling better?" I ask with concern.

She nods.

"Well, you missed a good time," Paige tells her.

I take a moment to really look at Paige in her lemon-yellow sundress, which is stunning against her sprayed-on tan. The tan's not too dark and has no streaks; just golden and healthy and realistic. "Your tan looks really good," I tell her. "Very natural."

"Thank you." She holds out her arms to admire them. "I finally found the best salon in town. This girl is a real artist and she uses several shades of dye to get these results." She extends a long tan leg, which sets off her white Louboutin sandals nicely.

"The tan is lovely, Paige." Fran nods. "In fact, you both should be sure to get yourselves sprayed before the Bahamas trip."

"Absolutely." Paige nods as well. "You should go too, Fran."

"I'll keep that in mind." Fran looks back at her notebook and I suspect that getting herself spray-tanned doesn't rank high on her to-do list.

"I want Mom to go in before the wedding," Paige tells me. "I scheduled her for Thursday."

Fran then pulls out her notebook and begins going over some details for today's show. I'm surprised Leah's not here to help, but at least Fran seems to be doing better than on Monday. I want to ask how she's feeling but don't want to tip-off Paige.

"As you know, the *Malibu Beach* camera crew will be there as well," she tells us. "But we have a verbal agreement that our show will take the lead."

"Hopefully Brogan agreed to that too," I say.

"She'd be a fool not to." Paige is polishing the lenses of her new Gucci sunglasses. The white frames look like old Hollywood, but Paige can pull it off. Add the sun hat that goes with her dress, and she looks pretty hot. I'm not so sure about *my* hat, but she told me it can be optional.

"Brogan should appreciate us being there," I say, knowing full well that Brogan will probably act anything but appreciative.

"You'd think she might even be nice to us—that is, if she wants her line to be a success." Paige chuckles as she slides her shades on. "Not that we can promise anything, since her fashion-challenged designs are not exactly stylish. And if she turns this show into a dramady, she might as well forget it."

"Just get a good show out of it," Fran says in a slightly tired tone. "That's all Helen wants."

"A good show ..." Paige makes a sly smile. "We'll do what we can, won't we, Erin?"

"I'll do my best." I slip the notes Fran gave me into the new Prada bag that I'm using today. It's from their summer line, a woven leather in shades of tan and white. It goes with my sandals, which are strappy and light-feeling with their tall cork platform soles. Thankfully, Shauna insisted on painting my toenails a peachy shade, which gives me a bit more polish and goes nicely with my peach and white floral sundress. I'm not as well put together as my sister, but I won't embarrass her either. Well, except for my pale skin.

One of our camera guys, JJ, is already in front of the posh

hotel with his camera ready to roll as our car pulls up. Paige gracefully emerges from the town car. And like she's a real star, which I guess she is, fans and paparazzi greet her.

"Go ahead," Fran tells me. "Just follow Paige's lead and I'll be along in a few minutes."

"Are you feeling okay?" I ask quietly.

"I think so." She presses her lips together. "Paige knows where you'll be seated and I'll be nearby."

"Okay."

"And if I have to visit the ladies' room, I'll have my phone."

"Are you sure you're—"

"I'm fine, Erin." Her eyes have a slightly hard look. "You just get out there and do your job, do what it takes to make this a good show, and I'll do mine."

"Right." I reach for my hat and purse and get out of the car, wishing I was as graceful as my sister. But no one seems to be noticing anyway, since all eyes and cameras are on her. She's fielding questions about her recent engagement to the popular designer Dylan Marceau.

"No wedding date yet," she says cheerfully. "We're not in any big hurry." Then she holds out her hand so the paparazzi can get shots of her big diamond ring. "I think a long engagement sounds like fun."

"What does Benjamin Kross think of all this?" a young woman calls out.

Paige shrugs. "I suppose you would have to ask him about that."

"So how does it feel to be rubbing elbows with the *Malibu Beach* crowd again?" another reporter asks Paige.

Paige smiles brightly. "I can't wait to see Brogan's new line of beachwear."

"And you're not worried that some of the cast, including Brogan Braxton, still bear some ill will toward you? Especially in light of the late Mia Renwick? You know Mia and Brogan were quite close."

"It's obvious by my presence here today that I harbor no hard feelings toward any of the *Malibu Beach* cast," she answers. "And, although I deeply regret Mia's death as much as anyone, I had nothing to do with the actual event. Brogan wouldn't have invited me to join her today unless we were on friendly terms." She flashes them a smile then links her arm into mine. "Now my sister and I are off to see what this new BBB line really looks like."

"Nicely done," I say quietly as we go into the hotel lobby, trailed by JJ and his camera. There I notice several people from the *Malibu Beach* crowd milling about. I'm surprised they're not in the show, but maybe Mollie was right about how they feel about Brogan. Like us, the *Malibu* girls are wearing sun-friendly outfits, but compared to Paige, I think they look rather frumpy and dowdy. As we walk by, everyone says hi, smiling and waving as if we're all good friends.

Paige leads the way, following the BBB signs out to the pool area, which is all set for the fashion show. Glistening glass patio tables with turquoise umbrellas and comfy-looking white chairs surround the pool, which is decorated with brightly colored floating flowers. There's a strip of white canvas running alongside the pool, and I assume that's supposed to be the runway. As a photographer, I'm thinking this is a nice setup. The models should look good with the blue water background.

"Very nice," Paige says as we take in the scene. JJ is rolling film and it appears Brogan has more going on than we assumed. Each table has a tropical flower arrangement and some seashells, along with placards with the guests' names listed. Really, it seems well planned and swanky in a beachy sort of way. An usher hurries over to escort us to a table up near the platform where I assume the models will enter the show. But, unlike the other tables, this table has no umbrella and it's in direct sunlight, which feels like about a hundred degrees at the moment.

Paige shakes her head. "No ... no, this will not do."

The usher looks surprised. "But this table is for you." He points to the placard with our names on it. "You *are* Paige Forrester, right?"

Paige looks around the pool area. The tables are starting to fill up, but there are still a few empty ones. "Over there," she says to the guy. And, realizing what she's up to, I pick up the placard with our name and follow her, and he follows me as Paige leads us to a table on the opposite side of the pool. I notice JJ is running his camera the whole time, but that's not unusual. It's always better to have too much film than not enough.

Paige stops at a table that not only has an umbrella, but is partially shaded by the palm trees behind it. She picks up the placard, which ironically has the names Benjamin Kross and Vince Stewart on it, and hands it to the surprised usher.

"I know these guys," she informs him in a familiar tone. "I'm sure they will totally understand this switch." She sets down her purse and points to an open area behind our new table. "And now there's room for our camera crew as well. This is perfect!" She flashes him her smile and thanks him profusely. He looks slightly star struck, and there's a spring in his step as he carries Ben and Vince's placard to the sun-baked table across from us.

"Much better," she tells me.

"Nice move," I say.

"Are you ready to do some behind-the-scenes filming now?" JJ asks Paige. "I think Alistair is already back there getting some footage of the models."

Paige points at me. "I think you need to stay out here and hold onto this table."

"Okay …" I nod, but I'm imagining a showdown with Brogan over her seating arrangement.

"Don't worry," Paige assures me. "It would be terribly bad manners for our hostess to try to bump us from our seats."

"Right."

Paige and JJ head into the tent-like cabana that's right next to the platform. I think it must be where the staging area and dressing room are set up. As I sit here feeling uncomfortable about our little table switch, I suddenly remember Mollie's warning about watching our backs. Then I realize that's pretty paranoid. Paige is right. Brogan wouldn't make a scene. Not with all these people starting to sit down.

As I wait for Paige, the music begins to play and drinks and appetizers are served. I take a sip of my strawberry lemonade and begin to relax. It's reassuring to see Fran sitting over on the sidelines in the shade, with a water bottle in hand. I hope she's okay. I'm tempted to go check on her, but don't want to abandon this table. So I wave, and she waves back.

Then I see Paige coming back out with JJ and Alistair on her heels. She is still smiling and looking fresh and pretty in a very classic Grace Kelly sort of way. I notice heads turn to follow her, and people chatting amongst themselves, no doubt about her. I realize, again, that my sister really has that "special something." And while I'm happy for her and somewhat proud, I always feel cautious too when all that attention is heaped on Paige. I've seen the whole fame thing turn on her. So has she. You never want to get too comfortable in the spotlight. It can burn you.

"Hey there," she says as she eases herself into the chair by me, gracefully crossing one leg over the other as a waiter scurries over, asking her what she'd like to drink.

She orders a Diet Coke then nods over to the hot spot table, which is still empty. "I'll bet those boys don't even show," she says to me quietly. "We could've been stuck sitting over there in the hot seats while this table remained vacant."

"You're probably right." But the words are barely out when I notice some familiar faces. "Don't look now," I tell Paige, "but Benjamin and Vince have arrived." Then my jaw drops.

"What?" she demands without turning to see.

I make a speedy recovery, pasting a stiff smile on my lips. "Oh, it's nothing. I'm a little surprised to see Blake is with them."

"Ben must've invited him."

"Yeah . . . right." I still have a hard time wrapping my head around Ben and Blake's friendship. Blake reached out to Ben after Mia's death, hoping to help Ben find God. And that's cool . . . except it doesn't seem that Ben is terribly interested in God. Sometimes I worry about who is influencing who.

"Poor Blake . . . stuck with Ben at that sweltering table." She gets a thoughtful look. "Hey, why don't you invite Blake to come sit with us?" She nods to a nearby chair. "We can make room."

"Oh, that's okay," I say quickly. "I think he'd rather be with the boys."

She chuckles. "Yeah, right. Baking in the sun?"

The guys are sitting down, and Benjamin seems to be positioning himself so that he doesn't look directly at Paige. They put on sunglasses and I suspect they're just realizing they got the worst table in the place. The expression on Benjamin's face is so disgruntled that I can't help but giggle.

"What is it?" Paige asks.

"It seems that Benjamin is not pleased with his table." Just then Blake looks directly at me and I want to crawl under our table. Instead I just smile and make a little finger wave. But as I do this, I feel like such a fake. I'm not even sure why, exactly, except that this whole scene is so not me. Dressing up like this, wearing a sun hat and shades, feels false, like I'm playing someone else. And then waving at Blake that way, like we're still buddies but knowing we're not. I'm about as authentic as Brogan Braxton. She's pretending to be a designer, and I'm just plain pretending.

Chapter
5

I'm still trying to shake that phony feeling when Brogan emerges onto the main platform. She's wearing a black sundress, which I have to wonder about—I mean, who wears a *black* sundress? Especially on a sweltering day like today. She takes a quick little bow, I'm not sure why. Then she hurries back into the tented area as if she's got some last-minute design issues to attend to, although I have my doubts. As she disappears, the emcee steps forward to the podium, welcoming everyone and gushing about how exciting the new BBB line is and how she can't wait to get this party started. Suddenly the music gets louder and the show begins.

I try to act interested, but besides the high-energy music, this show is nothing like the ones Paige and I are used to attending. Even the models, mostly people I recognize from *Malibu Beach*, seem substandard and unprofessional. There are a couple of missteps, and one girl stumbles over a wrinkle in the canvas sidewalk. She actually falls and loses a shoe.

That's bad enough, but it's these BBB designs that really make me uncomfortable. Sure, I'm no fashion expert, but if someone told me these outfits had come from BigMart, I wouldn't have been surprised. Not only do the materials look cheesy, but the colors seem garish, and I honestly wouldn't want to wear any of them.

I glance over at Paige, and although she's wearing her polite smile, I can tell by her eyes that she is even less impressed than I am. "How did you handle this backstage with Brogan?" I whisper into her ear, smiling as if I'm saying something nice about the hot-pink bikini and orange sarong that are strutting on the other side of the pool.

"It was so sad," she says. "I actually had to question Brogan on some things. You know, for the sake of the show."

I glance around at the other tables. Some people seem mildly impressed, but maybe they're mothers of the models and can't help themselves. Many others look how I feel — somewhat bored, a bit confused, and fairly disappointed. Still, I can't believe it when all the women at one table stand up, as if on cue, and leave. I'm not a BBB fan, but as much as I'd like to walk out, I would never do it. In fact, I think it's inexcusably rude.

As a girl in a striped red and green swimsuit struts by, I steal a glance to where Blake and the guys are sitting — and roasting — and feel a little stab of guilt. Of course, this is followed by relief as I realize that could've been us melting in the heat. Because even in the shade, it's toasty. I pick up my program, using it to fan myself, as if my being warm somehow makes up for the table swap. I then open the program and pretend to be highly interested in the content and notice there's an intermission. I hope it's soon.

A model wearing a purple and teal sundress does her final lap down the runway and the music slows down, suggesting it's time for a break. Several of the guests stand up and move about, and I wonder if they are about to make a getaway. Paige stands too, waving to the camera guys to come over.

"We might as well make use of this time," she says as JJ fiddles with her microphone. "That way we can leave as soon as it's over."

Alistair and JJ focus their cameras on her as she stands by the pool, critiquing what we've just seen. And, while she's not brutal, she is truthful. Some of the other guests come closer to listen.

"I do give Brogan Braxton credit for trying something like this," Paige continues. "Starting a new line of clothing is not for the weak of heart. And certainly Brogan's color choices suggest that she is a *brave* young woman. However, because Brogan *invited* me here to cover her design debut, and because I'm a bit of a fashion critic, and for the sake of my fans and viewers, I must be totally honest. BBB might appeal to, say, the tweener generation. But I doubt that anyone in the real fashion industry is going to take this line of beachwear terribly seriously. And I'm sure we won't be seeing her line at Bahamas Fashion Week." Paige smiles. "Of course, this is Brogan's first appearance on the style scene—as a designer anyway. And it's possible that she might surprise us down the line, but I have to say that here and today, it's not working for—"

"*Excuse me.*" Brogan seems to have appeared from no-where, and I'm wondering just how much of Paige's mono-logue she's overheard. Judging by her expression, Brogan's heard more than enough.

"Oh, hello, Brogan." Paige smiles brightly. "Here is our designer now."

"What are you doing?" Brogan seethes.

"I'm doing the monologue for my show. You know how our show works. I would've done it afterward, but I figured why not make the most of intermission and—"

Brogan points to where I'm sitting. "Why are you sitting at *this* table?"

Paige laughs lightly. "I'm sorry?"

"I asked you why you switched tables, Paige. *Didn't you hear me?*"

"I heard you, I was just taken aback."

"You and your sister were assigned to that table over there." She points over to where the guys had been sitting, but they are nowhere to be seen now.

"I don't see that it makes any difference," Paige tells her. "Besides, that table was rather hot."

"I had you seated there to give you a better view of the models coming out."

"Oh, I can see them just fine over here," Paige tells her.

"Yes, but that isn't the point."

I can see that Paige's patience is fading fast. "Then tell me, Brogan, what is the point? Did you want Erin and me to sit over there and suffer heatstroke from sitting in the glaring sun?"

Brogan feigns surprise, as if she had no idea the table was minus an umbrella.

"Because if that's how you treat your guests, after you asked us here to include The BBB on our show, well, perhaps we should excuse ourselves." Paige hands me her mic and gives me a "let's get out of here" expression. I'm already reaching for my bag.

"You just want to ruin this for me, don't you?" Brogan's eyes are narrowed as she steps closer to Paige. "First you mess with my seating arrangement—"

"I'm sorry," Paige interrupts. "I think the only one who can ruin this show is you, Brogan." Paige waves her hand toward the pool area. "And I actually felt hopeful when we got here. This is a great setting and you're doing a lot of things right." Paige steps onto the canvas runway by our table. It looks like she's trying to slip past Brogan gracefully in order to get her purse from the other side of the table, but Brogan is blocking her. "Unfortunately, there's a lot you're doing wrong too," Paige continues coolly. "And in the fashion world—"

Just then Brogan shoves roughly past her. In fact, she actually shoves Paige. And, as if in slow motion, Paige is teetering dangerously on the edge of the pool. I jump from my chair and attempt to grab her hand, but it's too late.

Paige, in her beautiful lemon-yellow sundress, topples right into the swimming pool. Alistair and JJ run to the edge, as if to help her, but seeing that she's okay, they continue to film the spectacle. With a furious expression, Paige sputters, and Brogan laughs. In that moment it takes all my self-control not to push Brogan into the pool as well. But, somehow, I can feel Fran's eyes on me, and I'm sure she expects me to salvage this fiasco—to keep it a good show and not just a free-for-all.

So, with everyone around the pool staring at this scene, some of them commenting and a few of them laughing, I grab the microphone that Paige just gave me and I nod to JJ as he continues to film. With mic in hand, I step closer to Paige and, facing the cameras, I begin to speak.

"It seems that Brogan Braxton was unable to make a splash of her own at her debut fashion show today." I tip my head to where Paige is peering up at us from beneath her drooping, dripping hat. "So she decided to use my sister to make a splash instead."

"That's right!" Paige nods eagerly.

"Are you okay?" I ask her.

Paige smiles. "You know, the water is actually quite re-freshing," she calls back to me.

"There you have it. My sister is ever the optimist." I turn to Brogan. "And it seems that Paige could give you some lessons in both etiquette *and* fashion."

Brogan looks like she's about to shove me into the pool now, so I take a few steps away from her, moving to the pool ladder, where Paige is climbing out. "So here we are," I say to the cameras as I give her a hand. "You've seen for yourselves what BBB fashion is all about today. And in my opinion Brogan Braxton Beachwear would not hold up in the water as well as my sister Paige Forrester is right now."

Paige, looking slightly drowned, smiles brightly as I hold the mic in front of her. "And if you think I'm all wet," she says as she removes her hat, wringing it out in front of the cameras, "you should check out these BBB fashions. Because seriously, fashion friends, I would rather go swimming in this little number"—she holds out her arms and strikes a pose—"than in any of the beachwear I've seen here today." Paige turns to Brogan, who is glaring at us like she wishes we were dead, and smiles. "Thank you for a very entertaining afternoon, Brogan. If your BBB line doesn't sell as anticipated, you might consider donating your originals. I hear the circus is coming to town."

Paige turns back to the cameras. "And now, fashion friends, remember to always put your best foot forward." She sticks out a dripping sandal. "Today that would be a rather soggy pair of Louboutins that I picked up in Paris last spring." She sadly shakes her head. "And speaking of Paris ..." She gives Brogan a quick sideways glance. "We will soon take *On the Runway* to the Bahamas. There we will show you some truly gorgeous beachwear that is worth paying attention to. So thanks for joining us for another episode of *On the Runway*."

Paige turns away from the camera to see that the other guests are still watching her. Their expressions are a mix— everything from confusion to shock to delight. Paige makes a deep bow for their benefit. The small crowd actually claps and some even cheer.

She waves her hand at the cameras. "That's a wrap, boys. Now let's get out of here before Brogan tries to push us all into the pool."

We exit the pool area and congregate in the lobby, where our crew expresses relief at having finished the show in half the time expected.

"This is going to make a great show," Alistair tells Fran. "We caught the whole thing on film."

"That's great," she tells the guys. Then she turns to me. "And good job holding it together, Erin."

"Thanks."

"Nice recovery," she tells Paige.

"Very nice," I agree. "Even with those raccoon eyes, you were a class act."

"Thanks a lot," Paige mutters as she grabs a compact from her bag and, peering into the mirror, starts repairing the damage to her mascara.

After we get home, I tell Mom about the BBB fashion show while Paige takes a long shower.

"You girls." Mom shakes her head as she fills a glass with water. "Such adventures!"

"Speaking of adventures," I say, "are you getting excited about Paris?" Jon had originally planned to take Mom on an Alaskan cruise for their honeymoon, but when he heard that Paris was her dream locale, he changed his plans. Now they will spend two weeks in France instead.

"I've had so much on my mind lately ..." She sighs. "I can hardly even think about Paris."

"You mean because of the wedding?" I ask. "Remember, you're supposed to rely on your bridesmaids for help with that."

"No, the wedding is looking good. It's work that's been consuming me. It feels like there's so much to get arranged before I'm gone."

"Don't you think Channel Five can survive without you?" I tease.

"Judging by some of the crew, you'd wonder." She sets the glass down. "Being a producer of a local news show is demanding. Sometimes I wonder if it's really worth it."

"Worth what?"

"You know, the stress, long hours ... all that goes with my job." Her brow creases. "I didn't really have a choice after your dad died. I had to take that job. But it's hard work. And sometimes I wonder ..."

"Are you thinking about quitting?" I ask.

"I'm not sure. I'd still want to work in television. But maybe I could find something less stressful. Jon's been urging me to think about it."

"I thought you loved your job."

"I *used* to love it. And I was thankful to have it. But, more and more, I'm just not sure."

"Well, after next week, you won't have to think about it for two weeks."

"I can't believe the wedding is only a week away." Mom gets a sad expression.

"Aren't you glad?"

She takes a sip of water then shrugs. "I guess so. But I'm a little blue too."

"Why?"

She waves her hands. "I'm going to miss this."

"The condo?" I frown. "You're going to miss this condo?"

She smiles. "No, silly. I'm going to miss you. And Paige. We three girls, living together."

"Oh . . ." I nod. "Yeah, I'm going to miss it too."

"You girls can change your minds and come live with Jon and me."

I press my lips together. We've had this discussion a number of times already, and we always end up at the same place. Paige and I agree we'd rather live in the condo on our own than move in with the newlyweds.

"I know," Mom says. "You and Paige need your independence."

"We'll visit you," I assure her, "and you'll visit us."

"Yes." She nods. "I know. It's just hard letting go of some things."

I go around the breakfast bar and hug her. "I know exactly how you feel. And you're not the only one I'm losing," I remind her. "Paige is going to get married too."

"Oh, that won't be for a long time," Mom says reassuringly.

"I hope so." I glance at the clock, surprised to see that it's after six. "Are you and Jon going out tonight?"

"He asked, but I told him that if you girls were staying home, I would stay home too. I thought we might enjoy a quiet Saturday night together. I can order some Thai food and maybe we can watch an old movie." She pauses. "Unless you were planning to go to your youth group tonight."

"I told Mollie I'd take her," I begin. "But she'll understand if I explain this is our last Saturday night together. I better call her."

Mom looks relieved. "And I'll order dinner."

To make up for not taking Mollie to fellowship group, I call her and tell her—in detail—about everything that happened at the BBB fashion show. I get her laughing so hard she tells me to stop. "You're going to make me go into premature labor," she says, "or wet my pants!"

So I bring my tale to an end. "That episode should be really good," I finally say. "I can't wait to see the footage of Paige standing there in the pool, her hat drooping and mascara running all over the place, and her saying calmly that the water is refreshing." We both laugh. As I hang up, I'm thinking my sister might've looked like a train wreck, but the girl has style.

Chapter
6

"What's up between you and Blake?" Mollie asks me as I'm driving her home from church on Sunday.

"What do you mean?"

"I mean, why are you avoiding him? Or is he avoiding you?"

"No one's avoiding anyone." I drum my fingers on the steering wheel.

"Yeah, right. I have eyes, Erin. I know they say you lose brain cells when you're pregnant, but I'm not totally clueless. Not yet, anyway."

"No one called you clueless."

"So tell me, what's going on with you two?"

"Nothing." That's true enough.

"Did you break up?"

"How can you break up with someone when you're not even going together in the first place?"

"Huh?"

"Blake and I were just friends, Mollie." I stop for the red light, wishing she would stop this inquisition.

"*Were?* Meaning you're not now?"

"No. I mean we are still *just friends.*" Okay, I'm not sure I believe that.

She gets stern. "Just tell me what happened, Erin."

I suspect by Mollie's tone that she's not going to settle for any more of my double-talk. "The truth is I'm not really sure what happened," I admit.

"Okay, then just start at the beginning."

So I explain how I told Blake that I don't see our relationship as being exclusive or committed . . . not now, anyway.

"You mean you think you'll want to take it to the next level someday?"

"I'm not sure. All I know is that I don't want to feel like we're that serious." The light changes and I try to act very focused on my driving.

"Why not?"

I shrug. "I don't know. Maybe I'm just not ready for *serious.*"

"I still don't get it, Erin. Don't you *like* Blake?"

"Of course I like him." I shoot a *duh* look her way.

"Okay, then do you *love* him?"

"I do love him. But maybe there are different kinds of love."

"Meaning you're not in love with him?"

I think about this. "Define what that means."

"You know what it means, Erin. When you're in love with someone you think about him all the time. You want to be with him. You miss him when he's gone. You don't want to live without him. You *know.*"

"Is that how you felt about Tony?" I turn and lock eyes with her for a brief moment.

Mollie gets quiet and I'm worried I've said the wrong thing again. All I need right now is for her pregnant hormones to start another crying jag.

"I'm sorry," I say quickly. "I know you loved Tony. And I thought he loved you too. Maybe that's another reason I feel confused about this whole love business. How is it possible to truly love someone—and then suddenly you don't? How does a person just turn off love?"

"I still love Tony."

"Oh ...?" I turn down her street, wishing I hadn't opened this can of worms.

"And I hate him too."

"Uh-huh?" I kind of understand this, and yet I don't totally get it. When I'm in love—if that ever happens—I want to be *wholeheartedly* in love. I don't want any hate mixed in.

"You *used* to love Blake too, Erin. He couldn't have broken your heart last year if you hadn't been in love."

"Okay ... I guess you're right." I pull up in front of her house, and once I put the Jeep in park I turn to face her.

"So my question is: Did you stop loving him?" Mollie asks.

"I'm not sure." I'm also not sure I want to answer this question.

"Or are you just *afraid* to love him, because you think he'll hurt you again?"

I press my lips together, trying to process her words. "I guess that's a possibility."

"You honestly *don't* know?" Mollie frowns at me like she's questioning my sanity, like somehow this should all make total sense. She wants it to be cut and dried, black and white. And I just don't see it like that.

"I'm not sure," I say again.

"Okay, then tell me this: How would you feel if Blake started dating someone else?"

"I . . . I don't know."

"Maybe you should think about it. Because Blake is a cool guy, Erin. And he's good-looking too. I'm guessing it won't take long before another girl comes along and sees that he's a real catch. And maybe she'll be ready for a serious relationship. What then?"

I take in a deep breath, slowly letting it out. "I really don't know, Mollie."

"I guess you'll just have to figure it out then."

Mollie invites me to come in, but I'm tired of this conversation and I make an excuse to go home. As I drive, I'm convinced that Mollie is blowing this whole thing out of proportion. Maybe Blake and I are both just taking a little break, putting our relationship on hold—a hiatus. What's wrong with that?

But when I get home and find a note saying Mom and Paige went shopping, I feel inexplicably lonely. I know I could call Mollie and do something with her. But, thanks to her pregnancy, her list of interests has shrunk considerably. I actually think about calling Lionel for one of our old photography excursions, except I suspect he has a new girlfriend. I've seen him with Lena twice now, once at fellowship group and today at church, and I don't think it's a coincidence. And, really, I'm happy for him. He's a great guy, but I never could imagine getting serious about him.

Finally, I decide to take my neglected camera and just head out on my own. When I was about twelve, my dad took me to the La Brea Tar Pits and I haven't been back there since. Today I plan to lose myself by shooting hundreds of pictures.

Thanks to my involvement in the show, my photography has suffered. I'm not even using my video camcorder as much as I used to. I rationalize that I'm getting great on-the-job training, but the truth is a part of me feels cheated.

But after an hour of shooting old fossils at the tar pits, I still feel lonely. This is the kind of place where you need someone with you, someone to talk with about these amazing things. So I put my camera back in my pack, get into my Jeep, and just sit there like a dummy. It's like I don't know what to do, like something is eating away inside of me, but I don't want to acknowledge it.

I know I'm feeling sorry for myself. For one thing, I've been thinking about the last time I came here . . . with my dad. And now he is gone. I should be over it, but there's still this dull ache inside of me. Like something is missing in my life. Dad was the one who really understood me — it's like if he were here, things would be better.

Then I consider how my mom will be remarried in less than a week. In a way, she'll be gone too. And I don't just mean on her honeymoon either. Oh, I know she sees it differently, but she's moving on. She will be giving Jon most of her time now. She obviously won't be living at the condo with us. I can't even quite imagine how that's going to feel. Mostly I'm trying not to think about it.

I think about Paige, and how she's engaged. Although she doesn't even have a wedding date yet, she feels partially gone to me as well. It's like she's here, but she's not. She's thinking about Dylan, planning for her wedding and her new life, which will most likely be in New York. Then she really will be gone.

I know it seems pitiful, but it's like I can't stop myself. I start thinking about Mollie, and the upcoming birth of her baby. Naturally, she's preoccupied. And I don't blame her. Once her baby arrives, I'm sure she'll be consumed by it. Even if I try to remain a part of her life, it's going to be different. It's like she'll be gone too …. gone from being my buddy to being someone's mommy. I can't even imagine it.

I'm thinking Blake is gone too. Maybe I did push him out of my life, though I don't think I really intended to do that. I'm kind of in shock that it even happened. He'd been so patient with me and then he abruptly just walked away. Maybe he decided I wasn't worth the effort. Or maybe Mollie is right, and another girl came along who treated him better than I did.

None of these observations make me feel better, but I think I need to face up to these things. I need to accept that I cannot control the people in my life. I can't freeze them in time like the prehistoric animals that got trapped forever by the tar pits. People will come and go, and there's nothing I can do about it. So I might as well get over it. Move on!

But I don't want to let go of loved ones. And having to let go of them makes me feel like giving up completely— like, why bother to have any relationships at all? If I don't let people get close to me, maybe I won't get hurt. And yet that thought makes me sadder than anything. I need people.

In moments like this, only one thing makes me feel better. And that's to pray. Which is exactly what I do. First of all, I tell God that I'm confused, and that relationships baffle me. I admit to him that my fear of getting hurt makes me want to push people away. If it's going to end badly, why even begin? I confess to God how lonely that makes me feel. Isolated and frozen in time—kind of like those prehistoric animals. I don't like it!

Then as I'm praying, I realize that God is right here with

me. He is the one relationship I can always depend on. No matter what, he does not leave me. He never will. That's a huge comfort. I'm not alone. Not only that, but I know God has good things in store for me—relationships that will be strong and healthy and good. I'm not frozen in time ... in fact, I need to keep moving forward to find them.

I'm about to start my Jeep when I remember Fran and what she's going through. I've been praying for her, but I wonder if I can do something more. I know Fran's not married and is currently without a boyfriend. Does she have family or friends around her? Or is she, like me, feeling lonely too? I take a chance and dial her number. Her voice is so weak and raspy that I'm sure I woke her.

"I'm sorry," I say quickly. "Were you resting?"

"No ... I was barfing."

"I'm sorry."

"Yeah. Me too."

"I ... uh ... I just wondered if you wanted any company."

"Company?" She sounds shocked.

"You know, someone to hold your hair when you're worshiping at the porcelain throne."

"So you figured that one out?"

"Yeah, it wasn't that difficult. Anyway, I'm just kind of doing my own thing today and I got to thinking of you, and I wondered if you needed someone to hang with."

"Really?" I hear a trace of hopefulness in her voice.

"Do you like frozen yogurt?"

"Yeah ... that actually sounds good."

"Any favorite flavors?"

"Maybe something fruity. Surprise me."

So I swing by Twinkles and get a raspberry and a peach

yogurt then drive over to Fran's apartment complex. I've only been there once and can't even remember which unit is hers, but seeing her little red car parked in a numbered spot tips me off.

"Come in, Erin," she calls after I knock. "It's unlocked."

I let myself in and, to my surprise, she's on the floor amidst a pile of cushions. And Fran looks, as Paige would say, like something the cat dragged in. Her hair is pulled back in a greasy ponytail, her sweats are grubby, her face is pale, and her lips are cracked and dry-looking.

"Are you okay?" I kneel down on the floor next to her.

"I've had better days." She explains how she's scheduled the chemo treatments during the end of the week and on the weekend so that she can work the other days. "Sundays are the worst."

"Feel like some yogurt?" I hold up the white bag. "Peach or raspberry?"

"I'll try some peach."

I take out the little carton, open it, stick in the plastic spoon, and hand it to her. Then I sit down, lean against the couch, and begin to eat the raspberry one.

"This is good," she tells me as she takes another bite. "Just what the doctor ordered."

"I'm glad." Then, because it's so quiet in here, I begin to talk. I tell her how I was at the tar pits feeling lonely and sorry for myself and how I prayed ... and how it felt like a God thing that I ended up here.

"Like you're my angel?" She makes a sad little smile.

"Or like God sent me." I take another bite.

Sighing, she sets the yogurt carton on the rug and leans back on the cushions, closing her eyes. "I'm glad he did, Erin."

She looks so tired and beat up. I wish there was something I could do to help, but this is all new to me. How do you help someone who's sick like this? I see her half-eaten yogurt and suspect that's all she can handle for now. "Want me to put the rest of your yogurt in the freezer?" I offer. "For later."

She barely nods. "Thanks."

I go into her kitchen, which is really messy, and put the yogurt in her freezer, which is surprisingly barren. I'm thinking Fran needs help. Just the same, I don't want to overstep my bounds, so I go back to ask her if she minds me cleaning up a bit, but she seems to be asleep. She also seems to be shivering, so I find a couple of throws and cover her. She doesn't even open her eyes.

Then I go back into her kitchen and start cleaning, throwing things away, loading the dishwasher, scrubbing down the countertop tiles and sink. Okay, it's not exactly my favorite way to spend a Sunday afternoon, but at the same time, it feels really good to help someone. Fran continues to sleep while I clean, moving from the kitchen to the bathroom, which is seriously in need. Fortunately, it's a small space that cleans easily.

After that, I timidly go into her bedroom, which smells so stale I go ahead and open a window. Then I strip the sheets from her bed, throw them into the washing machine, and remake her bed with fresh sheets. As I hurry to get as much done as possible before she wakes, I'm curious about Fran's life. Does she have family nearby? Or friends?

Finally, I think I've done about all I can and I'm surprised to see Fran's still sleeping. She is so quiet and motionless that I actually stand over her, staring hard to be sure she's breathing. Then, reassured that she's simply sleeping soundly, I return to her kitchen and open the fridge. And it's just as I thought—nearly as barren as her freezer. This is not good.

I quietly tiptoe out of the apartment, hurry to my Jeep, and drive to a nearby grocery store. Then I wonder ... what does Fran like to eat? I try to remember how it feels to have the flu. What makes you feel better? I pick out the kinds of foods I think my mom would try to get me to eat. I get different kinds of fruit juice, saltine crackers, chicken noodle soup, applesauce, a loaf of bread, some fresh fruit and vegetables, a couple more cartons of frozen yogurt, and a quart of milk. Enough groceries to fill two heavy bags.

When I knock on Fran's door this time, she actually opens it. "Oh, it's you again." She yawns sleepily. "I just woke up."

"I—uh—I got you some groceries," I say as I come in. "I hope you don't mind. It looked like you needed some things."

She blinks. "You got me *groceries*?"

"Is that okay?"

She looks like she's on the verge of tears. "Yes, of course. I'll get my purse and pay you—"

"Just let me get these into the fridge," I say as I go into the kitchen, setting the bags on the counter. "We can settle up later. Are you feeling better?"

"The nap helped," she says. "I was about to take a shower. I think I finally have enough energy."

"Go ahead and do that," I urge her. "I'll let myself out after I put these away."

"Thanks, Erin."

As I hurry to put things away, I realize that she didn't even notice that I'd done some cleaning. I guess that just shows how rotten she's feeling. It's like she's oblivious to her surroundings. Besides, I remind myself, I didn't clean to get her appreciation. I cleaned because it needed doing.

I can hear the shower running, so I decide to do a couple more things. I put the wet sheets in the dryer then quickly straighten her living room. And I write her a note, saying that I want her to call me if she needs anything and that the groceries are a gift. Then I leave.

I feel good as I get back in my Jeep. It's a cool thing to help someone like that. But as I drive home, another part of me is worried. I'm thinking maybe I should've offered to stay with her in case she needs more help. At the same time I know Fran is a private person and it's possible I've invaded her space enough already. In fact, by the time I get home, I'm hoping I haven't offended her by cleaning her apartment. What if she thinks that was my way of saying she's a slob?

Finally I decide that instead of obsessing, I should simply pray for her. And that's what I do. I am still praying for God to do a miracle in her, but I'm also praying that God will bring more people into her life. It's ironic, because there I was feeling sorry for myself because I was lonely. But poor Fran is not only facing a life-and-death challenge, she seems to be very much alone. In comparison, my life is absolutely full.

Chapter 7

Fran calls me at noon on Tuesday and she's very appreciative of my help last Sunday, which makes me feel good.

"You sound so much better," I tell her as I take leftovers from the fridge. "Maybe the chemo is really working."

"I feel pretty good today." She explains how her oncologist is using a "three days on, four days off" plan. "I get treatments on Friday, Saturday, and the last one on Sunday morning. So I only end up crashing on the weekends. Plus, my doctor thinks it's the best way to treat the cancer—three days of aggression and four days to recover and rest."

"So that's what you're doing today?" I ask. "Recovering and resting while you're at *work*?"

"Well . . . I'm taking it easy."

"You sure were wiped out on Sunday," I remind her.

"It was a rough day. But, really, I almost feel like myself today."

She does sound better, and I'm hoping her treatments are working. I want to ask her if Helen is getting suspicious yet, but I just hate rocking her boat. It seems so fragile and tippy already.

"Anyway, I'm on my lunch break and I'm going to take a quick nap. We've been putting together the tapes from Saturday."

"The fashion fiasco show."

"The footage is really hilarious. I think it'll be a good episode."

"Cool."

"In fact, that's why I'm calling. We scheduled a preview on Friday at ten. Can you let Paige know?"

"Will do."

I'm encouraged to hear Fran's feeling better, but I'm still concerned. Seeing her like that on Sunday was a little disturbing. Obviously, it was unsettling on a personal level because I really care about Fran. It was also disturbing on a professional level because I just do not see how she can maintain her job and her cancer treatment without derailing both. And when I think about the Bahamas trip coming up, I get seriously worried.

"Hey, you," Mom comes into the kitchen with her arms full of bags.

"Hi, Mom. What are you doing home this time of day?"

"I took a long lunch break to do some last-minute shopping. I'll make up for it this evening." She peers at me curiously. "You seemed like you were in a bit of a funk when I came in just now. Everything okay?"

I take in a deep breath, wondering how much I should say.

"Erin?" She cocks her head to one side. "Is something going on with Paige?"

It's ironic how she immediately goes to Paige when she

suspects trouble. And, in a way, she's not too far off the mark. "Not *exactly*."

Mom sets her bags and purse on the table then goes to the fridge to retrieve a yogurt and an apple. "What is it then, *exactly?*" She gets a spoon and a paring knife then sits down at the breakfast bar with an expectant look.

"I promised to keep it a secret," I confess.

Mom's brows arch as she opens the yogurt carton. "A secret about your sister? From your mother?"

"No, it's not a secret about Paige."

Mom looks evenly at me as she dips her spoon.

"Can I trust you, Mom?"

She smiles. "I am your mom, Erin. If you can't trust me, who can you trust?"

As she eats her yogurt and apple, I quickly pour out Fran's sad story, even the part about finding her in such bad shape on Sunday.

"Oh, poor Fran." Mom shakes her head. "That's devastating."

"I know. And I can't believe she's trying to work and do her treatments."

Mom gets a thoughtful look. "Sometimes work can be therapeutic, Erin. When your dad died, it was going to work every day that helped me get through some of the hardest times."

"I can understand that." I nod. "But I'm not sure Fran has the physical strength to keep up. The Bahamas trip is less than two weeks away."

"And Helen doesn't know?"

"No. Fran made me promise not to tell anyone. In fact, I feel guilty for telling you."

"Well, Fran should understand that. I'm your mom, after all—I have a right to know what's going on in your life."

"But you won't tell Paige?"

Mom frowns. "Actually, she has a right to know too. But, no, I won't tell her if you don't want me to."

"No, please don't say anything. And I don't want you to worry about this," I tell her. "I mean, you've got your wedding to focus on."

"Fran has put a lot on you with this, Erin. It's a heavy load to carry."

I give her a confident smile. "Because she trusts me with it. It's okay. I'll figure out how to handle it. I think it's a one-step-at-a-time thing."

"Maybe Fran will come to her senses and tell Helen what's going on soon."

"Or maybe, like she hopes, the chemo will work and she'll get better."

"Yes." Mom doesn't look convinced. "Hopefully that will happen."

"And, believe me," I say, "if I think Helen needs to know, I will tell her. It wouldn't be fair to ruin the show or Fran's health just to keep a secret."

"Good." Mom smiles. "I'm glad you can see that."

"I know you won't be back from your honeymoon when we're heading to the Bahamas, but I'll let you know what's going on."

"Yes, we will be like ships in the night. You girls leave in the morning and we get home that evening. But I'd appreciate being kept in the loop. You can always call me in France if you need to."

I laugh. "Seriously, Mom, what kind of daughter calls her mother while she's on her honeymoon?"

Fortunately, the week progresses without any complications or new developments with Fran. On Friday morning, when we're all in the screening room to preview the BBB episode, Fran seems almost like her old self and I'm thinking maybe she's right. Maybe she is going to beat this thing.

"Well, you girls really knocked that one out of the ballpark." Helen is beaming at us as the lights come on. "The viewers are going to *love* this."

"I didn't realize I looked so awful." Paige grimaces. "I'm not sure I want that image going public."

Helen laughs. "It's a little late for that. Didn't you see that shot of you on *E!* last weekend?"

"Don't remind me." Paige shakes her head.

"Hey, it's publicity," I tease.

"And you handled it extremely well," Helen assures Paige. "You both did. I'm proud of you girls."

"Do you think we'll take any heat for dissing BBB?" I ask Helen as we head to the conference room to continue this discussion.

She chuckles. "Well, I doubt they'll be lining up to be a sponsor, but I suspect we were a little rich for their blood anyway."

Once we're resettled in the conference room, Fran opens her notebook. "We still need to get some more monologue critiques from you," Fran tells Paige. "To go with the actual fashion show."

"And I can be totally candid and honest?" Paige asks Helen.

"In a dignified, ladylike way," Helen tells her. "We want to keep Paige Forrester on the high road."

Paige nods. "This is going to be fun."

"Maybe you should help," Fran tells me. "Can you come up with some good comments?"

I grin at her. "Oh, yeah, I had some opinions."

She turns to Leah. "Why don't you get them scheduled for next week?"

"I'm on it." Leah gathers her things and leaves.

"So are you girls excited about your mom's big day tomorrow?" Helen asks as the four of us linger in the conference room. Paige gives her a blow-by-blow of everything we have to get done by then. Hearing the to-do list, I'm actually feeling overwhelmed.

"Maybe we should let them get on their way," Fran says to Helen.

"Sounds good." Helen nods. "I think we're done here."

"Are we still okay with JJ getting some footage *after* the wedding?" Fran asks us. "During the reception?"

"Absolutely," Paige assures her. "In fact, I've hired JJ to tape the wedding ceremony as well."

"We'll combine it with the wedding dress shopping as well as the wedding dress fashion show," Fran explains to Helen. "For a wedding special that will play in late June."

"Wonderful!" Helen claps her hands.

"You're both still coming to the wedding, right?" Paige asks them.

"You bet." Helen smiles. "I'm a sucker for a good wedding."

Fran nods. "I'll be there."

We all head our various ways, but as Paige and I are about to split up in the parking lot (she insisted we come separately because there's so much to do today), she hands me a list.

"What's this?"

"Your to-do list for the day."

"Okay ..." I glance over the list, which isn't too overwhelming and is mostly what I thought I was going to be doing anyway. And then I see it ends with Acapella's. I know Acapella's is a swanky salon, but I'm not sure why I'm going there at four thirty. "Am I supposed to pick up something at Acapella's?" I ask.

"I scheduled appointments for all three of us several months ago."

"Really?"

"Yes! Won't it be fun?"

"Sure. But will we be late for the rehearsal?"

"My plan is that we'll go directly from Acapella's to the rehearsal. So make sure you take what you want to wear with you."

"Okay."

"Maybe you should tell Blake to pick you up at Acapella's. I'll just take Mom with me."

We reach her car, and I just don't want to go into the recent events with Blake and why he won't be with me tonight. So I nod and smile instead. I can explain later. Besides, Paige will be going stag, or whatever girls call it, tonight too. Maybe she and I can get in some sister time together.

I run around town, doing last-minute things that should've been done last week. When it's nearly four, I'm thinking a couple hours of pampering at Acapella's is sounding pretty sweet. So I swing by the condo, grab my dress and shoes for tonight, and just as I'm going down the stairs, Grandma Hebo is coming up.

"Grandma!" I shriek happily.

We hug, and she explains that she's on her way to the hotel where some of our other relatives are staying and where tonight's rehearsal will happen. I tell her I'm on my way to the salon and that Mom and Paige are there too.

"Well, come on down and meet someone before you go," Grandma tells me. She leads me to a car where an older man gets out, and my grandma introduces me to Howard Stack— *her boyfriend*!

I try not to act shocked, but I cannot believe my grandma has a boyfriend. This is so out of the blue. "Nice to meet you," I say as he shakes my hand.

"I'm looking forward to meeting the rest of your family," he says politely. "I've heard such good things about you."

"And he watches your TV show," Grandma tells me. "In fact, I've actually seen it a few times myself."

"But you don't have a TV," I point out.

Howard chuckles. "That's how we got connected. She wanted to come over and use my TV."

"So we could say that you and Paige brought Howard and me together."

"Interesting." Then I apologize and tell them I have to run. "But I'll see you tonight at the rehearsal dinner."

They wave and I hop into my Jeep, where I simply shake my head. My grandma has a boyfriend. That is just crazy.

Mom and Paige are already at Acapella's when I arrive, and before long we're all being manicured and pedicured and coiffed and pampered. As the stylists work, I tell Mom and Paige about Grandma Hebo's boyfriend. Naturally, this brings on speculation and humor, and it feels like we're three old girlfriends just out having a good time.

"I could do this every other day," Paige says as we're all relaxing in the big leather recliners at the pedicure station.

"I feel so spoiled," Mom admits. "But I like it."

By six thirty we are finished with our appointments and in the dressing room getting ready for the rehearsal. Paige's phone rings, and suddenly she is jumping up and down in her underwear, squealing like she's won the lottery.

"What is it?" Mom asks as Paige hangs up.

"Dylan!"

"Yeah?" I peer curiously at her. She doesn't normally do the Snoopy happy dance when Dylan calls.

"He's here."

"In LA?" Mom blinks.

"He made it after all. He's on his way here to pick me up. So I won't be the only one without a date at dinner tonight after all." She frowns at Mom. "I was going to give you a ride to the—"

"Oh, I forgot to tell you, *my date* is picking me up." Mom looks at her watch. "I'd better hurry. Jon said he'd be here by six forty-five."

"And Erin's going with Blake, so I guess we're all set."

As we scramble to get dressed and do our final primping, I just can't bring myself to tell them that Blake won't be at the dinner tonight. For one thing, they'll want to know why. And then they'll probably feel sorry for me. I just don't think I can deal with all that in seven minutes or less, so I say nothing.

But I am determined not to feel sorry for myself tonight. This is about my mom and Jon, and I don't want anything to put a damper on it. At the rehearsal, when I'm asked where Blake is, I simply say that something came up and he couldn't make it tonight, but that he will definitely be at the wedding tomorrow. No one seems to question it. And, as far as I know, since he was invited, he will be at the wedding tomorrow. He just won't be *with* me.

The rehearsal goes fairly smoothly. We all realize it will be a bit different at the rose garden in the park tomorrow, but this was the best we could do for an evening rehearsal. For the dinner afterward, also in the hotel, I sit with Grandma and Howard, who fortunately don't know anything about Blake, so there are no sticky questions for me to answer.

Instead we talk about cameras and photography. It turns out that Howard has been taking photos for decades and has just recently decided to step into the digital world. I'm thankful for the distraction of explaining all the latest, greatest technology to him. Because, frankly, I'm practically the only one here without a date tonight, and it feels a little lame.

Chapter
8

On the morning of Mom's wedding, I call Blake. "I need a really huge favor," I tell him.

"What?" He sounds like I woke him up.

"I know we're not together, but last night at the rehearsal dinner, my mom seemed concerned about me being alone. Dylan arrived yesterday for Paige, and even my grandma has a date. I don't want mom getting worried if it looks like you and I aren't speaking to each other. I just don't want to be that one gray cloud on her otherwise sunny day. You know? So, I'm begging you, Blake, could you please just *act* like you're with me today?"

"Okay."

I'm surprised but relieved. "Okay then. Well, thanks. I appreciate it. I just don't want Mom heading off to her honeymoon all worried that I'm back home dying of a broken heart." I instantly regret that last bit.

"Not that there's any chance of that," he says wryly.

I let that comment pass. "So do you want to just meet there then?"

"Works for me."

As I thank him again, I can't help feeling like I just hired an escort. Really, how dumb is this? Maybe I should've just told my family the truth. What difference does it make? Or maybe it's my pride ... maybe I'm embarrassed to be dateless at my mom's wedding. But if that were the case, why didn't I just call someone else? There are plenty of guys in our college fellowship group who would willingly escort me to a wedding.

"Erin," Paige is calling to me. "Come help me with this."

And that's how the morning starts and keeps on going—Paige calling the shots and me answering. By one o'clock we have ourselves and our mother pretty much together, and we're actually not feeling too stressed. Mom looks elegant in her satin dress and pearls, her hair swept up in a French twist, her makeup done perfectly by Paige.

"The limo will be here in about ten minutes," Paige tells Mom.

"A limo?" Mom blinks.

Paige grins. "You bet. We are going out in style."

I'm opening the chilled sparkling cider that Paige insisted we must use to toast with before leaving the condo. I fill three champagne glasses, hand one each to Mom and Paige, then start the first toast.

"Here's to the best mom ever," I say, "and to all the good times we've had together. And here's to many, many more!"

We clink glasses and sip, and then Paige makes a toast. "Here's to a great marriage with a great guy." She winks at Mom. "And to a great honeymoon!"

"That reminds me," I say suddenly, "I was supposed to have your bags at the door for the driver to take down. Are they in your room, Mom?"

"Wait," Mom says. "I need to make my toast."

So I pause as Mom raises her glass. "Here's to the two best daughters any mother could ever want. Here's to your careers and your futures. May they be as bright and beautiful as you two are."

We have a group hug and try not to cry. The next thing we know, the driver is knocking on the door and we're scrambling to get Mom's bags and gathering up the miscellaneous things that need to go to the rose garden with us. Finally we're almost out the door, but Mom stops, takes one last look inside the condo—almost as if seeing if for the last time—then closes and locks the door.

"It's the beginning of a new era," she says in a serious tone.

Then to brighten the mood, I begin to sing "Here Comes the Bride," and Paige joins in as we troop down the stairs in our wedding garb. But as we're getting into the white limo, I see tears in my mother's eyes. So Paige and I make small talk as we ride. Paige talks about details in regard to the wedding. I tell Mom about some of my favorite spots in Paris, although I've already written them down for her. I think we're mostly just trying to fill the air, keeping things light and happy. I know I'm having a hard time holding back the tears.

But once we're at the garden, we're distracted with getting ready, and soon the ceremony begins. The wedding goes fairly smoothly, thanks, I'm sure, to Paige's meticulous planning. It is so beautiful in the rose garden. My mom was right to pick this place. The roses are in full bloom and the golden afternoon sunlight filtering through the trees is magical. And when I see Jon slip the ring onto Mom's finger and look into her eyes with that expression of pure devotion on his face, I feel sure she's in good hands.

Then I see Mom's face, just before they kiss, and she looks radiantly joyful. That's when I give up trying to hold back my tears. Paige and I are both crying, but they're happy tears. Mom has had so much sadness in her life that it would be impossible not to be glad for her now. I even think my dad is happy, and I feel him with us.

After the wedding and some photos in the rose garden, the wedding party relocates to the hotel where the reception is being held in a ballroom. Although the wedding was small and intimate, and I think absolutely perfect, Paige convinced Mom to invite more guests to the reception—as well as to pull out all the stops. And when Mom protested that it would be too expensive, Paige and I offered to cover the expenses. It's not every day that daughters get to pay for their mom's wedding reception.

I'll admit that I wasn't too thrilled about this reception idea at first, mostly because Mom had been dragging her heels, but now that we're here and I see all these people together—all of Jon's and Mom's TV industry friends, plus ones that Paige and I invited, as well as old friends and family—I realize this is one fun group of people.

Blake is keeping his word by pretending to be "with" me. We sit side by side at the main table, smiling and acting congenial, but in reality we are barely speaking. We're like actors playing roles, and I can tell he's not enjoying it any more than I am. Then, after toasts are made and food is served, the dancing begins. Paige worked it all out: Mom and Jon dance to "The Way You Look Tonight," which is so romantic. After that song ends Jon invites Paige to dance, and Mom invites Jon's only son, Robert, to dance. Then they break midway and Jon asks me to dance. Meanwhile Paige asks Dylan. By the third song, I'm expected to ask Blake to dance, so I do.

"Thank you for cooperating with this," I say to him with a stiff smile.

"You're welcome." He matches my smile with one that's equally stiff.

"You're a good sport and I appreciate it."

He just nods.

"And if you want to take off early, I'll understand."

He gives me a curious look. "So ... are you asking me to leave?"

"No, of course not."

"But you'd rather I wasn't here."

"I didn't say that, Blake."

"You didn't have to."

We continue to dance in silence now. I'm so frustrated I can't even think of anything to say. Part of me wants to ask him why he is acting like such a jerk. Another part wants to tell him I'm sorry. Instead, I do nothing. When the music ends, Blake formally thanks me for the dance, makes an elaborate bow, and walks out of the ballroom. I glance around to see if anyone witnessed our mini drama, but thankfully everyone seems more interested in their own dramas ... or rather, romances.

Mom and Jon are dancing again, and Paige is cheek to cheek with Dylan. Even my grandma and her boyfriend are cutting the rug. Yes, I feel a little left out, but since this is my mom's big day, I am determined not to give in to self-pity. That's when I remember Mollie. It's not like she has a date today either. I look around the room until I spot her sitting along the sidelines with an older woman that I don't recognize.

"How's it going?" I ask her.

She points to her plate. "The food's good." Then she introduces me to Jon's Aunt Betty from Utah. But after a few minutes of small talk, Aunt Betty excuses herself to go to "the little girls' room."

"Guess it's just you and me," I say to Mollie. I laugh and start singing, "Just Mollie and me, and baby makes three, so happy are we——"

"Yeah, yeah," she interrupts. "Real funny, Erin."

"Sorry, I couldn't resist."

"You look really pretty." She points to my dress. "That color looks good on you."

"Thanks."

"And the wedding was really beautiful." She sighs and rubs her tummy. "If I ever get married, I want to do it in a rose garden too."

"I know. The light was so gorgeous, I was actually wishing for my camera during the ceremony."

"So what's up with Blake?" Mollie looks around the room. "Is he still here?"

"I think he left." I let out an exasperated sigh.

"What happened?"

I tell her the short story and she just shakes her head. "I guess that proves you don't love him after all."

"What do you mean?" I demand. "How would that short conversation prove anything?"

"I mean, why do you think Blake asked if you wanted him to leave?"

I shrug.

"That was his way of asking you to beg him to stay."

"I don't think so, Mollie."

"You are so dense."

"Thanks."

Mollie pushes herself to her feet.

"Are you going to dance?" I ask.

She laughs sarcastically. "Yeah, I'm going to waltz all the way to the restroom."

"Maybe you can tango with Aunt Betty in there," I tease. After she's gone, I start to feel conspicuous sitting here by myself. Something about being a bridesmaid alone on the sidelines feels a little embarrassing. I look around for someone else to talk to and spot Fran on the other side of the room. Like me, she is alone.

I go over and sit down by her. "How's it going?"

She sighs. "I was actually thinking about making a getaway, but I came with Helen and Frank and they're out there doing the boogie-woogie."

I laugh. "The boogie-woogie?"

She makes a weary smile.

"So why don't you grab a taxi and go home?" I suggest. "I can make up some excuse to Helen for you."

She looks relieved. "Would you mind?"

"Not at all."

"I actually have a date."

I blink. "A date tonight?"

"It's tomorrow. But it's a morning date so I need to get up early."

"A breakfast date?" I frown at her. "Who with?"

"Chemo." She reaches for her purse.

"Oh ... does anyone go with you?" I ask.

"You mean to hold my hand?" She's standing now, unsteadily. For a moment she teeters and I worry she might fall over.

"Yeah." I nod as I stand and link arms with her.

"No ..."

I give her a cheesy smile, in case anyone is watching us, then walk her out of the ballroom and to the elevators.

"I wish I could go with you," I say as I walk her through the lobby. "I really think you should have someone there."

"It's okay. I'm fine. I'm used to being on my own."

"Don't you have any family around?"

"No. They're all back East."

"Any good friends?"

She turns and looks at me with sad eyes. "When you marry your job, you tend to lose your friends."

We're outside now, and I ask the doorman to call her a taxi. "Well, I'm your friend," I tell her as the taxi whips up. "And if it wasn't my mom's wedding, I'd go with you right now to make sure you got home safely."

"Thanks, Erin. I appreciate it. But, really, I'm fine."

I watch as the taxi leaves. And, as bad as I feel about Blake, it's hard to feel sorry for myself in comparison to Fran.

I return to the reception wearing my happy face. I mix with the crowd, visit with old friends and family, meet some of Jon's relatives, dance with Mollie, and finally make an excuse for Fran to Helen. "She forgot she had a date at five," I tell Helen.

"A date?" Helen looks interested. "With whom?"

"Someone with a Hawaiian name," I say. "Like Kimo or Nimo, I think."

Helen chuckles. "Who knew?"

Finally the reception crowd starts to thin and it's just close family and friends, visiting and finishing off the champagne. Then it's time for the happy couple to leave for the airport.

We all go down and, instead of throwing the bouquet, which seems silly since there are only a few of us left, Mom hands it to Paige. Then she kisses us, and she and Jon get into the limo and take off.

"Wow." Paige shakes her head. "It's over."

Dylan puts his arm around her waist, pulling her close and pointing to the bouquet in her hands. "That one's over, but this one is just beginning."

She giggles then turns to me. "Hey, where's Blake? Dylan and I wanted to take you guys to dinner. I already made reservations."

"Blake had to go check on something," I say offhandedly. "Why don't just the two of you go out tonight?"

Paige smiles at Dylan. "I guess we could do that."

He grins back and I can tell there will be no argument.

"Do you have a way home?" she asks me.

I nod. As they go their way, I ask the doorman to call me a taxi. The older man smiles as he waves a car over. "Such a pretty young woman riding alone on a Saturday night." He makes a *tsk-tsk* sound. "It's like that old line."

"What line?" I venture.

"Youth. It's wasted on the young."

I laugh and thank him. As I get into the taxi I consider his words. I also wonder if perhaps I am fated to be alone. Perhaps there's some personality flaw that I'm unaware of that is unraveling my relationships. Not that I've had so many relationships, but it seems that whenever a guy gets even slightly serious about me, I push him away. I've heard about people, usually guys, who are afraid of commitment. I wonder if I might have that problem myself.

But as I pay the driver for my ride, I think that I'm being

ridiculous. Good grief, I'm barely nineteen and here I am worried about being single for the rest of my life. Seriously, that is so messed.

As I go into the condo, very aware that Mom is gone — really gone — and that Paige is out with her fiancée, I feel very alone. I'm tempted to call Blake and apologize. But for what? I'm not even sure.

Instead I take off my dress and put on comfy sweats and tell myself to just enjoy this — I have the condo to myself. I can turn up the music loud, or watch any movie I like. I could even take off my clothes and dance naked. Okay, I wouldn't want to do that. But all I can think about is how lonely I feel.

I look at the clock and see that it's just a little past seven. I imagine everyone else is out having a great time. Yes, I know that's not true, but it's how it feels. I remind myself that Mollie went home from the reception with swollen feet and a plan to take a bath and go to bed early. And then there's Fran . . .

I grab my phone and call her number. As it rings, I get ready to leave a message, but then she answers. "Fran?" I say eagerly. "How are you?"

"I . . . uh . . . I'm okay."

"Really? No ill effects from your chemo?"

"Just the usual stuff."

"Do you want any company?"

"Seriously?"

"Yeah. The truth is, I'm feeling lonely. Paige and Dylan went out. Mom and Jon are on their way to Paris."

"You know I'm not good company . . ."

"I know."

"You're welcome to come over."

"Are you hungry for anything? Like frozen yogurt? Or whatever?"

"You know what sounds good, Erin? Pad Thai."

"Pad Thai? Like the noodles?"

"Yes. For some reason, that sounds good."

"Pad Thai is on the way." I call in an order to a nearby Thai restaurant, gather up some overnight things, write Paige a note, and head out.

It's not that I'm helping Fran just to make myself feel better, although I'll admit that in some twisted way her health challenges make my problematic personal life seem trifling. I'm helping Fran because I know she needs it. And because it's the right thing to do.

Chapter
9

When I come home from Fran's place the following afternoon, I know I've made a big mistake. Not in helping Fran, because she was so sick I have no idea what she would've done without me. No, my mistake has to do with Paige. *And Dylan.* Somehow, it seems they've gotten the idea that it's okay for Dylan to stay in the condo this week.

"It's no big deal," Paige assures me when I notice the signs that Dylan did indeed spend the night last night.

"It's a big deal to me," I tell her. "This is my home too. You can't go moving your boyfriend in —"

"He's my fiancée, Erin. We are going to be married."

"But you are not married *now*." I glance toward the bathroom where Dylan is showering. "And Mom would not approve."

"Mom doesn't live here anymore. Remember?"

"Paige, this is just unfair."

"Erin." She's using her big-sister voice now. "I know you're very conservative about these things and I respect that. But we are not the same and —"

"That's for sure!"

"And I would appreciate it if you would respect that we're different."

I press my lips together. "This is just wrong, Paige."

She nods. "Yes, it would be wrong for you. But it's right for me."

I want to scream now. I want to pull out my hair and scream. Why does she not get this? This is my home. She is bringing in a guy without even caring how I feel about it. This is so wrong! Wrong. Wrong. Wrong.

"By the way, Erin ..." She looks at me curiously. "Where did *you* spend the night last night?"

"Huh?"

She holds up the note I left her yesterday, informing her that I was *visiting a friend*. "Who did *you* spend the night with?" She gives me a very suspicious look.

Now I feel trapped. How can I possibly explain that I spent the night at Fran's without giving Fran's secret away?

"And I know you weren't at Mollie's, because she called this morning, wanting to know if you were picking her up for church or not."

"Oh ... church." I nod, remembering now that it's Sunday, and while I was cleaning up vomit from Fran's hallway carpet, church was in session.

"So my guess is you were with Blake." She makes a catty smile. "I have no idea what you and Blakey-Boy were up to all night, but I have to say I'm surprised. I thought you didn't approve of that sort of thing."

"For your information, Blake and I broke up."

She blinks. "Seriously?"

And now, whether it's fatigue or stress or real sadness, I begin to cry.

On the Runway

"I'm sorry, Erin." She hugs me. "I didn't realize you guys broke up."

"I didn't want Mom to know," I sob out. "I didn't want to worry her just as she was going on her honeymoon."

"Was it a mutual breakup?" she asks as she goes to the kitchen and gestures for me to come along.

"I'm not even sure," I confess, following her. "I mean, it happened so quickly."

"Was it at the wedding reception?" She fills a glass of water. "I saw you two dancing and then I didn't see Blake again." She hands the water to me with a sympathetic expression.

I can only nod as I take a sip.

"Do you still care about him?"

"I—uh—I don't really know. I'm trying to figure it all out."

"Hey there," Dylan calls as he comes into the kitchen wearing only a bath towel. Then he sees me and looks embarrassed.

"I gotta go," I tell them, running to my room. I close the door, but I can hear their voices. I'm sure Paige is telling him that I'm upset and brokenhearted and who knows what else. And, while all that's true, most of my angst revolves around two things: one, I hate that Paige thinks it's okay for Dylan to stay here, and two, I'm worried that I almost blew Fran's cover just now.

I hurriedly pack some bags. There is no way I'm going to be comfortable staying in the condo with Paige and Dylan as they play house. I am so outta here.

"Where are you going now?" Paige asks as I emerge from my room with my bags.

"To Mollie's," I tell her.

She simply shrugs and I suspect she's relieved to be rid of me. And to show her how I feel about the situation, I slam the door on my way out. Real mature, I know. But I can't help myself. Then I drive to Mollie's and am received almost as warmly there as at home. .

"You could've called me," Mollie tells me as we go down to her basement bedroom, which I helped her paint and redecorate several weeks ago. I'm surprised that it still looks cheerful and sweet. Not a bad place to live, really. "I was all ready to go to church and then you never came."

"I'm sorry."

"My mom even offered to drive me, but by then I knew I'd be late and have to sit alone, and I just figured, why bother?"

"I'm really sorry, Mollie." And for the second time today, I start to cry.

Mollie's eyes get wide. "*Erin?*"

"Sorry—I'm just having a—really hard day."

"*What's wrong?*"

I tell her about Paige and Dylan playing honeymooners at the condo and how I just don't feel comfortable staying there.

"You can stay here with me."

"Thanks."

"That's why you're so upset?"

I sit down on her sofa and wonder … how much can I tell her?

"It's something more, isn't it?" She sits in the rocker and waits.

I sigh then nod.

"What?" she asks eagerly. "Tell me."

"It's supposed to be a secret."

"You can trust me, Erin. I'm your best friend, right?"

I nod again. "But I promised not to tell."

"Who did you promise? Blake? *Paige?*"

I lock eyes with her. "Do you promise, if I tell you, you won't tell anyone?" I think about this. Who would she tell? Although she does enjoy the whole social network scene.

"I swear." She holds up her hand. "Scout's honor."

"I mean it," I say grimly. "You can't tell anyone, Mollie. A person's life could be at stake."

"Seriously?" Now she looks really interested.

"Kind of seriously. Promise me you won't tell anyone. And no Facebook or Twitter or anything like that."

She puts her hand on her stomach. "I swear on the life of my baby, I will not tell."

"Oh, Mollie, you don't need to go that far. Although I appreciate that you see the seriousness of this." I tell her about Fran. At first she actually seems a little disappointed, like she wanted the secret to be something juicier ... more gossipy. That irritates me. So I go into detail about how sick Fran actually is, how she's getting chemo and vomiting and totally miserable, and how she doesn't even have the energy to open a can of soup.

"That's rough." Mollie rubs her belly. "I can relate on some levels." She reminds me of how she had morning sickness really bad.

"And now Fran's hair is starting to fall out," I add. "In big clumps. And we're supposed to go to the Bahamas in less than two weeks."

"Oh no!" Mollie's hand flies to her mouth. "That *is* really sad. *Poor Fran!*"

I try not to react to the fact that it took hair-loss issues to get to Mollie, but I do feel somewhat appalled.

Now Mollie looks confused. "But why are you telling me?"

"Because that's why I didn't make it to church. I spent the night at Fran's and Paige assumed I was with Blake."

Mollie chuckles. "Well, that just shows how little your own sister knows you."

I roll my eyes. "She knows me. She was just trying to get my goat because I was so ticked about her and Dylan shacking up."

"Shacking up?" Mollie lets out a hoot of laughter. "Who even says that?"

I shrug. "Anyway, I told Paige I was coming to stay with you."

"And so you are."

"But I think I might have to go help with Fran."

Mollie looks disappointed. "Doesn't she have any friends or family of her own?"

"Not really."

"Oh."

"So I was hoping you could cover for me. In case Paige happened to call here, which is highly unlikely since I'll have my cell phone, but if it happened and if I was at Fran's, you could somehow, without actually lying, cover for me."

"I guess so." She frowns. "I still don't get why you don't want Paige to know. Why is it okay for you to know, but not her?"

I explain how I found out. "Fran never would've told me. And she doesn't want anyone to know because she really needs her job. And you know Paige—if she knew about this, she'd throw a fit. Fran's not stupid. She knows she'll have to quit if the word gets out."

"How can she do her job when she's so sick?"

I close my eyes and lean my head back. "I ... don't ... know."

"It's going to come out in the open eventually, Erin."

I open my eyes at this. "Yes. Probably so. But Fran is so hopeful. She has her treatments on Friday, Saturday, and Sunday so she can work during the week. And she actually pulls it off ... kind of. Her job is everything to her, Mollie, and I'm afraid if she loses that, well, she might just give up."

"Wow."

"So, anyway, I want to help her as much as I can. If it looks like she really can't handle the Bahamas trip ... well, I'll deal with that when the time comes."

"That's a heavy load to carry."

"Well, I did tell my mom. But I swore her to secrecy."

"You know, I think it's cool you're helping her, Erin."

"Really?"

"Yeah. It's the Christian thing to do."

"I've really been praying for her."

Mollie nods. "I'll start praying for her too. And if there's anything I can do ..." She frowns at her big belly. "Which is probably unlikely given the condition I'm in ... but if there is, let me know."

"Thanks." I tell her about how I took Fran to her chemo treatment and back to her apartment a couple hours ago. "I only went back to the condo to grab a change of clothes, because I think I need to spend the night with her again. I'm afraid today's chemo is really going to knock her off her feet."

"Well, when Fran feels better, which I hope is soon, you're welcome here." Mollie smiles hopefully. "I would actually enjoy the company."

When I make it back to Fran's I discover that my prediction was spot on. Unfortunately, she's as sick as a dog. The new anti-nausea drugs aren't working and she's so wiped out that I honestly fear for her life. But when I ask about calling the hospital, she shakes her head. "Wait," she gasps. "It will pass."

By around three in the morning, it does pass, at least enough for her to finally go to sleep. Feeling fairly whipped myself, I clean up a few messes that I know can't wait until morning and then crash in her guest room. But when the sun is barely up, I hear Fran dry heaving again.

I do what I can, but I honestly feel like I'm in way over my head. If my mom weren't in Paris, which she should be by now, I would be calling her for help. As it is, I am on my own. Somehow I manage to get Fran to eat a small bowl of Cheerios and milk. She sleeps soundly until noon then miraculously gets up, takes a shower, gets dressed, wraps a stylish scarf around her head, puts on makeup and jewelry, and says she is going to work.

"Not without me, you aren't."

She blinks. "You can't suddenly become my escort in the workplace, Erin. People will get suspicious."

"No they won't." I shove my feet into my sandals. "I'm going to be your new intern."

"My intern?"

I nod and reach for my bag. "I actually would like to learn about production."

She looks at me as if a light just went on. "You know, that's not a bad idea at all."

"Yeah." I grin at her. "I thought of it myself."

As I'm driving Fran to work, I'm thinking maybe I've found the silver lining in this dark cloud — for me anyway. I'll get some hands-on training in television production, something that already interests me anyway, and Fran will get some much-needed help.

Chapter
10

After Dylan returns to New York, Paige and I seem to be having a standoff. We avoid each other, barely exchange words, go our separate ways. I don't even bother to tell Paige where I am when I don't come home. I know that's immature on my part, but the truth is I'm irritated at my sister. I think it was extremely selfish of her to let Dylan stay in our condo. So when I go AWOL, I actually hope she's worried, although I'm sure she assumes I'm at Mollie's, and most likely she doesn't even care. She's probably happy to have the condo to herself. It seems like she's in her own little world anyway.

I'm still helping Fran at work, and I spend the next weekend at her apartment. I drive her to chemo treatments, cook and clean, get groceries, and do everything I can to help her get through this. She's got a couple of wigs now and an appointment for a spray-on tan next week, and she's still determined to make the Bahamas trip, which is in just over a week. I don't know what to think.

On Sunday, after her last chemo appointment, I'm tempted to ask the medical professionals if it's safe for her to travel, but I know that would be stepping over the line. So I keep my mouth shut, reminding myself that she'll have the rest of the week to get stronger. And maybe by Saturday, with no chemo treatments to drag her back down, she will finally turn that corner to a real recovery like she's hoping. It may be unrealistic, but it's what I'm praying for.

"If you were Catholic, I'd think you were applying for saint-hood," Mollie tells me on Wednesday night. I'm sleeping over at her place, and I've just given her a progress report on Fran.

"Very funny."

"Seriously, Erin. You're like Fran's lifeline. Does she appreciate it?"

I shrug. "Sometimes she does. Sometimes it seems like I'm just aggravating her." Like today, when Fran got so cranky in the editing room that I just had to go do something else.

"Maybe being sick makes her moody," Mollie suggests as she removes a puffed-up popcorn bag from the microwave. We're watching an old movie tonight. "You know how out of sorts I can be with this pregnancy sometimes."

I only smile. No way am I answering that one.

"So are you and Paige speaking yet?"

"Not much." This is an understatement.

"Won't that make your Bahamas trip a bit awkward?"

"I don't know. Paige and I have had our ups and downs before. I'm sure we'll work this out by then."

"Does that mean you've forgiven her?"

I consider this. The truth is, I've been waiting for her to apologize to me. But I have a feeling there might be flaw in my reasoning.

"Because you know you'll have to," Mollie persists as she pops open a ginger ale.

"I know." I grab my soda and put the DVD in, eager to end this conversation and get lost in an old flick. I know I'll have to deal with Paige ... later. Why obsess over it now?

The next day, as we're going into the studio for a final strategy meeting for the Bahamas trip, which is only two days away, Paige is especially snooty to me.

"Nice to see you could make it here today," she says to me as we meet going into the building. "Nice outfit." I can tell by her expression that it's not a genuine compliment. And when I look at my slightly rumpled jeans and T-shirt, I get it. Still, it's not like I took a special wardrobe over to Mollie's with me. And it's not like we're filming today.

"Thanks," I say in a cool tone. We walk silently past the executive offices, and I'm thinking this meeting is not going to go well. As we enter the conference room I ask her, "So ... why wouldn't I make it here today?"

She gives me her innocent smile, the fake one. "Oh, I don't know. It's just that you seem to be running around quite a bit lately. I thought maybe you'd forgotten all about the show."

Fran and some of the crew are already in the conference room, and Fran looks curiously at Paige and back at me. "Doesn't Paige know you've been interning for me?" she asks in an irked tone. I can't tell if she's irritated at me or at Paige.

"Erin hasn't been home since our mom got married," Paige says lightly as she takes her usual place at one end of the table. Helen always takes the other end, and sometimes it's hard to tell which of them is really running this show.

Fran gives us a blank look, as if my comings and goings don't concern her in the least. I try not to take offense.

"I haven't forgotten our show," I say to Paige. "In fact, I've learned a lot about it by working in the editing room these past two weeks. Maybe you should try it sometime too. It adds a whole new perspective to—"

"I think my perspective is working quite well, thank you very much."

JJ chuckles. "Sounds like the sisters are having a squabble."

Paige gives him a big smile. "Not me. I'm not squabbling with anyone."

Helen comes in right after Paige's comment, and the focus changes to the upcoming trip. While Fran isn't as animated as she used to be in the BC (before cancer) days, she seems to be holding her own. I notice her forehead beading with perspiration though, and she's drinking a fair amount of water. I wish I'd thought to bring some raw almonds. Those seem to help with her nausea. I also wish that Leah were here to help carry Fran's load, but it sounds like she's tied up in the office taking care of last-minute arrangements.

Finally the meeting winds down and the crew, who will be flying out tomorrow to set up ahead of our arrival, excuse themselves. Now it's just Fran, Helen, Paige, and me.

Helen clears her throat then looks at Paige and me with a creased brow. "Is something bothering you two?"

Paige just shrugs.

"I haven't been home much lately," I say to Helen. "Maybe Paige has been missing me."

Paige laughs sarcastically.

"Does this have anything to do with your mother being gone?" Helen adjusts her glasses, studying us closely.

"Maybe," I admit. "I doubt that Paige would be doing the things she has if Mom wasn't out of the country."

Helen's brows lift and she turns her attention to Paige. "*Meaning?*"

Paige shoots me a warning look. "Meaning Erin doesn't know what she's talking about."

Helen nods to the open door, and Fran gets up to close it. "I want to know what is going on with you girls, and I want to know now." Helen's expression is grim. "Out with it."

I look nervously at Paige, wondering why I even opened my mouth.

"Erin?" Helen points her finger at me. "Talk."

I give Fran a helpless look, as if I think she can help.

"I think the girls are going through a transition period," Fran tries. "It seems only natural."

Helen looks as if she's considering this.

"And it's true I haven't been home. I've been staying with my friend Mollie," I say to Helen. "She's in her final trimester of pregnancy and she gets lonely."

"Oh . . ." Helen nods. "And perhaps Paige is missing her little sister?"

I try not to laugh.

"I've been lonely too," Paige admits. For some reason I almost believe her. "Erin hasn't been checking in with me at all."

"Is Erin expected to check in with you?" Helen asks. "I mean, since your mother is gone?"

"Well . . . we haven't really established rules." Paige twists her mouth to one side. "But maybe we should."

Helen turns back to me. "Paige makes a good point, Erin. Although you're both adults, it's still important to have accountability when sharing a home. No matter how old you are."

"That's true." I nod, but I'm feeling like the scapegoat here.

"And it's a two-way street." Fran directs her comment to Paige.

"I know." Paige almost sounds contrite. "I'll try to do better."

For some reason this is encouraging. Like she's taking some of the blame, although I still feel most of the fault is hers.

"So, friends again?" Helen asks hopefully.

I force a smile. "Of course. We're sisters, we have to be friends."

Helen laughs as if she knows better. Paige gets out of her chair, comes over, and makes a production of hugging me.

"I still love you, little sister."

I act like this is fine, but underneath my smile, I feel even madder now. I'm halfway tempted to just spill the beans, but it's hard to break the code of sisterhood—no matter how badly I want to. Plus Paige would simply shrug it off, since "being engaged is practically married" in her mind. Even so, I wonder how Helen and Fran would react if they knew about Paige and Dylan's tryst at the condo. After all, Helen has warned Paige to protect her reputation, to keep it clean—would she care that Paige cohabited with her fiancée last week? Or would Helen simply look the other way and chalk it up to normal behavior for engaged couples? After all, this is Hollywood. Really, who do I think I'm fooling?

"I thought you were going to get a spray-on tan." Paige frowns at me. "You're going to look like a brunette albino next to me."

"As a matter of fact, I made appointments for both Erin and me for tomorrow morning," Fran informs Paige.

This is news to me, but I smile as if I knew.

"Well, girls, I wish you the best in the Bahamas," Helen says as she gathers her papers and slips them into her brief-case. "I wish I could join you, but my schedule will simply not allow it." She shakes her finger at both of us. "And I expect you two to bury the hatchet and pull off some excellent shows over there. Because, as you know, this is *not* an inexpensive trip." She smiles. "Thank goodness our sponsors believe in this show. Let's not do anything to disappoint them."

Fran leaves on Helen's heels, and now it's just Paige and me. "Let's not do anything to disappoint them." I mimic Helen's final words.

"What do you mean by that?" Paige glares at me.

"Well, I'm just not sure how Helen, or our sponsors, or the network would feel about their starlet sleeping with her boyfriend."

"*Fiancée*," she says firmly. As if that means they're married.

"Fine. *Fiancée*. How do you think they'd react if they knew?"

She shrugs. "They'd probably take it in stride, Erin. It's how things are."

I frown. "You're probably right."

Her expression softens. "Look, Erin, I'm sorry I offended you. I've had time to think the whole thing over and I decided that it really was unfair for me to have Dylan stay at the condo."

"Honestly?"

"Honestly. It won't happen again."

I blink. "I really appreciate that."

Paige gives me a hug that feels sincere. I hug her back. "I hate feeling like we're enemies," I tell her.

"Me too." She smiles in a slightly catty way. "You know what else I hate?"

"Huh?"

She looks down at my clothes. "That outfit."

"Hey, I was in a hurry this morning. Mollie and I stayed up really late last night watching old movies."

"Yeah, well, it shows. Are you working with Fran today?"

"I can if I want, but I don't have to."

"Want to go shopping for some Bahamas clothes?"

"Won't they be provided as usual?"

"Yeah. But that doesn't mean we can't pick up a few things anyway. Come on, it'll be fun."

I realize that Paige's concept of "fun" is different than mine, but at the same time my life hasn't been much fun lately. The truth is, I have been missing her … and Mom. "Sure," I say. "Unless you're embarrassed to be seen with me like this."

She studies me. "Yeah … maybe we should swing by home first."

So we go home and I take a quick shower while Paige picks out my outfit, which turns out to be pretty cool. A silk, sleeveless BCBG top in a black-and-white print over a black cotton-blend skirt. But, as usual, it's the accessories that make it. A pair of Louboutin cage platform sandals in black.

"Those are pretty tall for me," I say as she presents me with the rather stunning pair of shoes.

"Try them, you'll be surprised."

So I try them and I am surprised, they're not as uncomfortable as I expected. Must be the platforms. And I must admit, it's fun being taller. Even so, I sneak a pair of flip-flops into the bright yellow Kate Spade bag she insists is perfect. When I check myself out in her mirror, it is perfect.

Before long we're just two sisters out on the town, shopping, having a late lunch, and reminiscing about the details of the wedding.

We don't really buy much, and on our way home I thank her for inviting me to go with her. "It really was fun," I admit.

"It was," she agrees happily. "And you know, Erin, I don't

want anything or anyone to come between us. You know that, don't you?"

"I think I do."

"Not even Dylan. *Okay?*"

"Okay …"

"And even though he'll be in the Bahamas—"

"He'll be in the Bahamas?" I demand.

"Sure. Dylan's got a resort wear line too. Those shows are a big opportunity for him. You wouldn't expect him to miss it, would you?"

"No, of course not."

"And even if Dylan and I do spend some time together there, which I know we will, I don't want that to come between us, Erin. I don't want to fight with you anymore."

"I don't want to fight either."

"Good. I'm glad we agree."

But as she drives us home I'm wondering what I just agreed to. I think it was something snuck in between the lines, and I have a feeling I just told Paige I have no problem with her and Dylan being together, or more explicitly, *sleeping* together. I realize it's none of my business. Not really. I mean, it's her life. Even if she is my sister, she has to live it the way she thinks is best. However, I don't have to agree with her.

Because, call me old-fashioned or conservative or whatever, but for some reason I still find it disturbing that she is willing to jump into bed with Dylan simply because he put a great big diamond ring on her finger. I wish Paige wanted to save that part of herself until *after* the marriage. But maybe I'm one of the few people remaining on the planet, or at least in this country, who feels that way.

Chapter 11

On Friday night, I find I am thinking about Blake. To be more accurate, I am obsessing. Suddenly I'm worried—what if he really is the right guy for me and I've pushed him away? Equally troubling is the idea that I have hurt him. I'm not even sure how, exactly, since didn't he dump me, but I keep remembering the look in his eyes when we danced at my mom's wedding. He seemed wounded, and that makes me feel lousy. I wish I could do something about it. Especially before we fly off to the Bahamas in the morning.

I consider calling him, but it's already past midnight. I'd send a TM, but that seems so impersonal—and email, well, that just feels wrong. So I decide to do something really old-fashioned. I'll write him a real letter. I pull out my best stationery and begin. Then I wad up the page and begin again. After three bad starts, I decide that no matter how this version turns out, I will not throw it away. I will continue until I'm done. I can always decide not to send it.

Dear Blake,

I'll be in the Bahamas tomorrow, but I really wanted to talk to you tonight, which is why I'm writing this. I'm not really sure where to begin and this is actually my fourth attempt. So bear with me. First of all I want to tell you I am sorry. I know I hurt you and, although I'm not exactly sure how I hurt you, I want to own up to it and apologize. I would never intentionally hurt you, Blake, because I consider you one of my dearest friends. And the truth is I really miss your friendship.

But, as you know, I've been conflicted over the whole dating thing for months now. I always question myself about how close is too close ... how intimate is too intimate ... whether to be exclusive or committed or not to be ... and so on. You already know about all this because we've had those conversations. And I know I've frustrated you, Blake. But you've always been patient with me. Until recently, that is.

Apparently your patience has run out, or else I simply pushed you away. I'm honestly not sure which one it is. Maybe it's both. But I wanted to tell you, from the bottom of my heart, that you have been a very special person in my life. I'm grieving the loss of our friendship. And I'm questioning a lot of things about myself and why I am the way I am—and whether or not it's good. I know I have some issues, some fears, some inhibitions, and things that I need to face. I want to deal with them, or at least acknowledge them. I don't want to be alone my whole life. And loneliness is something I've been giving a lot of thought to lately. I worry that I might be destined for loneliness. That disturbs me.

Anyway, I think I'm rambling now. The purpose of this letter was mainly to say I'm sorry to you, and also to say thank you for the friendship we've had over the years. As well as to say I miss you, Blake. More than you know. I understand your need to move on from me. I don't blame you one bit. And I wish you the very best.

Sincerely,
Erin

I'm not sure why, but I feel close to tears as I seal my letter in an envelope, address it, stamp it, then pack it in my carry-on bag. I'm unsure as to whether or not I'll even mail it. But somehow it feels like a load's been lifted, like I can sleep better knowing I've taken this step.

The morning is a mad scramble. Paige thought I'd set my alarm and I thought she'd set hers. As a result, both of us are still asleep when Fran calls from the limo, which is down in the parking lot. Fortunately, our bags are already packed, or mostly. We throw on some clothes and hurry down to the waiting car.

"I hope there are no paparazzi at the airport," Paige says as she opens her carry-on and starts doing her makeup and hair on the way to LAX.

"If there are, I'm sure you'll look fabulous," I assure her.

"It wouldn't hurt for you to run a brush through your hair," she shoots back at me. "And some lip gloss and mascara could do wonders."

I glance at Fran, and she nods.

"You're sure looking good," I tell her.

She smiles. "Thank you. I feel good."

I try not to seem surprised. "Great."

"Yes." Paige looks at Fran. "Your spray-on tan gives you a nice healthy glow." She turns to me. "Both of you. It's too bad sun is so damaging to skin when it makes us look so good." She looks more closely at Fran. "Have you lost weight?"

Fran shrugs.

"Well, whatever it is, you look fabulous."

I press my lips together, looking out the window, where I see that the gray dawn is just beginning to lighten around the edges a bit. When I think of how Fran lost weight, by puking

her guts out for the past several weeks as a result of her che-
motherapy treatments, it makes me want to scream.

We get to the airport and without any drama, paparazzi,
or security mishaps make it to our gate with about twenty
minutes to spare before boarding. Fran offers to sit with our
bags while Paige and I peruse the newsstands. As I'm returning to the gate, I see a mailbox. Why not send Blake his letter?
After all, it's only an apology. No reason not to send it. So I
hurry and get it from my carry-on, and as they're announcing
that it's time to load first class, I run back to the mailbox and
drop it inside. Done.

Of course, after we're loaded on the plane, I second-guess
myself. Maybe I shouldn't have sent it. What did it really say?
If it had been an email, I could go back and reread it and make
sure it sent the right message. As it is, it's gone now. No getting
it back. So I say a quick prayer, asking God to help my letter
to make sense—and to not hurt Blake even worse than I've
already done. And, as usual, I ask God to protect us on this
flight. Then I lean back and try to get some sleep.

After a long but uneventful flight, we land in Miami, where
we switch planes. Then after a much shorter flight, we arrive
in Nassau just before five. The air terminal is buzzing with the
fashion crowd. Paparazzi are all over, and when JJ and Alistair
pop up to get our arrival filmed for the show, they are joined
by others who may or may not know who we are. For the sake
of our crew, as we make our way from baggage pickup to our
waiting car, Paige makes observations, pointing out various
personalities and fashionistas who've also just arrived in Nassau, and some of the other cameras stay with her too.

Then, as if the light just went on, one of the journalists yells out to Paige in a thick Italian accent, asking her if she's *the* Paige Forrester of *On the Runway*. Naturally, Paige smiles and tells the woman that she's right and that we're here to film some shows as well as to participate in *Britain's Got Style*.

"Is it true you are no longer with Benjamin Kross?" the journalist asks. "You left him for a *designer*?"

"It's true," Paige tells her as we go out to the street.

"Oh, that is too bad." The woman shakes her head. "Benjamin Kross is so hot."

Paige just laughs then tells them we have to go, and we start piling ourselves and our luggage into the car. But once the doors are closed she lets out a sigh. "I forgot that Benjamin Kross is still a big deal in some countries ... the ones still watching old episodes of *Malibu Beach*."

"Publicity is publicity," I remind her.

Fran just nods, but I can tell she's tired. I can also tell that her wig has slipped, ever so slightly, but enough for my style-savvy sister to notice. So I point to some models just getting into a van and ask Paige who they are. Then, while she's distracted, I quickly straighten up Fran's do. Fran looks weary but grateful, and I know that if she doesn't hit a bed soon there will be a meltdown.

Fortunately, we go straight to the hotel, where I get a bell-hop to assist with our bags. Then I help Fran check us into our rooms, making sure that I get a room that adjoins with hers. Once I'm in my room, I knock on the adjoining door and wait until Fran opens it. She is minus her wig now. This was a bit startling last week, but I'm getting used to it, although her scalp looks strangely white and slightly alien-like in contrast to her sprayed-on tan.

Ignoring this, I help Fran into bed then call room service and order her a fresh fruit and cheese platter and plain turkey sandwich. While waiting for that to arrive, I make her some chamomile tea then unpack for her. I stick around until room service arrives and I'm fairly sure she's going to be okay.

"Thank you, Erin," she tells me in a bone-tired voice. "I promise I'll be back on my feet tomorrow, and I'll kick it into high gear by Monday."

I nod. "I know you will." But my thoughts don't line up with my words. I'm worried that she's even worse than last week. Oh, she might not be vomiting and all that, but there is something in her eyes, a weird kind of blankness, that tells me she's not getting better yet … and this trip is not going to help. But what can I do?

I'm barely back in my room when my phone rings.

"Let's get dressed to the nines and go out on the town," Paige chirps cheerfully on her end. To be honest, it's the last thing I want to do at the moment. Except that I know Dylan won't be here until Monday, and the idea of Paige going out solo and probably clubbing is a bit unsettling.

"Okay," I agree. "But I haven't even unpacked yet."

"So, get with the program, Erin."

"Well, for starters I need a shower and—"

"And I'll come help you get dressed."

"Thanks, but I think I can handle that—"

"No, I mean I'm bringing you an outfit, Erin. Our wardrobe is already in my room, and I'll pick out something for you."

"But we're not filming tonight," I point out.

"Don't be silly, Erin. We can still be caught on camera. You can't spend time around the Bahamas Fashion Week crowd looking like a slob."

I want to debate this but decide it's not worth it. "Okay. Give me ten minutes for a shower, then come over."

"I'll call for the car to pick us up at eight," she says.

I take my ten-minute shower and exit the bathroom to find Paige knocking on my door. "You forgot to get us adjoining rooms," she chides me as she comes in with an armload of clothes.

I act like I'm surprised to see that my room connects with Fran's. "We'll be okay like this, won't we?"

"I guess." She lays her load on my bed. I have to admit that after being with Fran, it's refreshing to be with Paige. I do love her sunny disposition, and the girl knows how to have fun. By the time she's helped me with my hair and makeup and has me dressed in a cool but sophisticated yellow-and-black Chanel dress, I feel like I'm ready to make a night of it.

"Two stylish single girls on the town," she says as we check out our images in the mirror. In a way our looks complement each other. She's the tall blonde beauty, I'm the petite brunette ... but somehow it works. "What about Fran?" she asks as she picks up her coral-colored Gucci bag, which goes perfectly with her coral Gucci sandals.

"She's having dinner in her room," I say. "I think she wants to go over next week's schedule." That's actually true. She does. The problem is she's too tired to do it tonight.

"Okay, then let's —"

"I, uh, I just have to use the bathroom," I say quickly, deciding I should check on Fran. "How about I meet you in the lobby in about five minutes?"

"Okay. I'll do some people watching while I wait."

I laugh. "More than likely, people will be watching *you*." As if to ensure this, Paige checks herself out in my mirror again, pats her hair, and retouches her lips. As usual, she looks perfect in the well-tailored sleeveless white Chanel dress.

"Fine by me." She laughs, adjusts her bag, then heads out. As soon as I know she's gone, I slip into Fran's room and see that she is sleeping soundly. I turn off most of the lights, just leaving the one near the bathroom on. I write a little note saying Paige and I have gone out, but that I have my cell phone if she needs anything.

As I ride down the elevator, I feel like I'm living a double life: part-time nurse maid, part-time fashion diva. I think if I had to do this for long, it might mess with my mind. For now, and for Fran's sake, I know I must keep it up. But it feels strange when I sense people actually watching me walk across the lobby—as if they think I might be somebody. And it feels doubly weird when I realize this is *the* fashion crowd.

When I join Paige, who is standing by the fountain and checking her iPhone, I know we're being watched. Rather, *she* is being watched. Dressed so classically and uptown, she's pretty hard to miss, even in this crowd. I've noticed that when they're not working, most models tend to dress pretty casually. Maybe it's because they spend so much time getting dolled up that they just need some down time. Or maybe they're as fashion-challenged as I am and could actually use some style advice.

"Hello, dahling," I say in a phony European accent. "You look absolutely mahvelous."

She gives me a sleek smile. "Same back at you, babe."

"Ready to rock and roll?"

"Oh, yeah."

I try not to giggle as we head out of the hotel, where paparazzi are snapping photos of anyone who is anyone as they come out the door. Actually it's a sign that hotel staffers are doing a fairly good job with security by keeping the riffraff out of the building. Paige smiles and waves as she gracefully climbs into our waiting car. I try to imitate her.

Do I feel like a celebrity? Maybe a little. Mostly I feel like an imposter, or like I'm riding my sister's stylish coattails. But as we ride to our destination, a popular hot spot Paige has picked out, I feel unexpectedly appreciative of this excursion as well as this experience. Even if our moment of fame is just that—a moment—I think when it's all said and done, I will be thankful to have been here.

Chapter 12

Fran doesn't seem to have any more energy on Sunday than she did last night. "I thought you'd be starting to feel better by now," I say as I pour her a cup of green tea.

"I thought so too." She's sitting on her bed with a pink scarf tied loosely around her head. She's wrapped in the comforter and shivering, even though the temperature in here feels about the same as outside, in the eighties. I point to her untouched breakfast tray. "You really need to eat something."

"I know. It's just . . . I have no appetite."

I sit in the chair across from her, literally wringing my hands. "What can I do to help you, Fran?"

"I don't know." There's a waver in her voice and I can tell she's close to tears. "I guess you were right."

"I was right?" I frown. "About what?"

"I shouldn't have come."

"Oh." As much as I normally enjoy being right, this makes me feel lousy. "Maybe you're just having a bad day," I suggest. "You know how that can go."

"Maybe … but it's been a whole week since I've had chemo. I shouldn't be having a bad day."

"Well, yesterday was tiring." I sigh loudly. "I'm even a little worn out. It's a good thing we have today to catch up."

"Yes." She nods sadly.

"So maybe if you eat a little breakfast, just your toast and fruit, and if you keep resting … by tomorrow you'll feel better."

"Yes." She makes a stiff smile. "I think you're right."

"Paige wants me to go shopping and do the beach thing with her today."

Fran waves her hand. "You go. Have fun."

I'm torn. It's hard to leave her like this when she looks so miserable.

"Go on, Erin. And, if you don't mind, take one of the camera guys with you to get some footage of you two just having fun. Okay?"

"Okay." I hold up my iPhone. "Call me if you need me."

She barely tips her chin in a tired nod.

"And drink your tea." I point to the cup by her bed. "Call room service for lunch, even if you don't feel like it."

"Thank you, *Nurse Erin.*"

I roll my eyes. "Hey, I just want you to get well."

"I'm trying."

But as I return to my room, I'm wondering — is she really trying? I know that's harsh, and I'd never say it to her, but I want her to get better and I just don't get it. If she wants to get well and strong, why can't she at least *try* to eat some food? Maybe something in her stomach would help with the nausea. At least Fran should get lots of rest today. Hopefully that will do the trick.

"You ready?" Paige calls from the hallway. I grab my things, and we are off … at least until we reach the lobby, where I remember what Fran said about filming. So I tell Paige and reach for my phone, hitting speed dial for JJ's number.

"Let's do the beach shots first," he tells me after I fill him in. "The sun will be perfect now." We agree to meet there, and I inform Paige that shopping will have to come later.

We head to the dressing room area by the pool, get into our suits, and then go out to the beach, where I see that JJ is already getting set up. Not too thrilled with the idea of being filmed in a bathing suit, I am wearing a bright-yellow sarong, as well as a navy-blue oversized straw hat and matching sunglasses. Naturally, Paige is making fun of my outfit. "You look like an old lady, Erin."

"Thank you," I say primly. "Maybe no one will recognize me."

"At least take off the sarong," she urges.

"No way." Even though I insisted on a one-piece suit, which sounded safe, this yellow-and-navy-striped number has french-cut legs that go nearly to my hipbones. And although the V-neck clasps with a silver metal buckle, it seems to be rather low and I suspect cleavage is showing. Then again, I could be exaggerating this whole thing in my mind.

"Is it because you're not comfortable with your body?" she asks.

"I am perfectly comfortable with my body," I tell her. "I'm just not perfectly comfortable having the whole world see this much of it."

She laughs as she adjusts a string on her pink and yellow bikini top. I shake my head; compared to my sister I probably do look like an old lady, but honestly, her bikini is so scanty I almost wonder why she even bothers. Although I'm glad she does. I've heard there are some nude beaches in the Bahamas. Hopefully, we won't be shooting on any of those. If so, I will positively decline!

"The sarong's okay," JJ assures me. "The colors are great, and your suit actually makes a nice contrast with Paige's ... uh ... outfit." He suddenly looks embarrassed.

"You mean Paige's *lack* of an outfit?"

He chuckles as he lifts his camera.

"Hey, you'd better get used to it," Paige tells him as she strikes a starlet pose with one hand behind her head. "Tomorrow we're covering a swimsuit shoot, and you are going to be seeing a lot of skin there."

It turns out we're seeing a lot of skin here at the beach today too. After a while, I do feel slightly overdressed in my "granny sarong," as Paige is calling it. But as long as the camera is running, I'm sticking to my guns.

"You know, Erin, you're probably not helping one of your favorite causes," Paige tells me as we're wading in the waves.

"What favorite cause?"

"You know, the whole body image thing?"

"Huh?"

"Well, if you're afraid to let America see your body because you're worried you don't look like a fashion model, you're cheating our viewers out of seeing a regular-looking girl who's comfortable in her own skin."

I consider this, and as much as I hate to admit it, Paige has a good point. The truth is I am more modest than my sister, but it's also true that I'm not that comfortable in my skin. Especially now, with so many thin model-type girls roaming around on this beach.

"Fine," I say as I untie the sarong. "You win." I turn and face JJ, who is still filming us. "This is for all you girls out there who worry about not looking like a model. I don't look like one either. We need to just get over it and be thankful that we are the way we are. So there!"

"That was good," JJ tells me. "Could you do it again, this time with the mic?"

And so, feeling a bit silly, I take the hand mic and do the whole thing again. Only this time my sarong falls into the water and I nearly drop the mic. "Oh, well," I say to the camera. "I'm sure you get the point. Let's stop focusing on overly thin girls with breast implants and start remembering that everyone is different. It's okay to just be yourself."

Paige is smiling and clapping now. "Bravo!"

I hand the mic back to JJ then pull my soaked sarong out of the water, wring it out, wad it up, and toss it at my sister. Before she can get me back I turn and run into the water, continuing until I'm waist deep and can dive right into the next wave. The water feels cool at first, but I quickly get used to it and swim out a ways, which I know will thoroughly aggravate Paige, because ever since she got tumbled by a wave as a child, she's scared to death of swimming in the surf.

When I come back, Paige is settled on one of the hotel lounge chairs, holding a green drink that's complete with a little orange umbrella.

"I'll assume that's a virgin something," I say as I sit down on the lounge chair beside her.

She simply nods then flips a page of her French fashion magazine.

I towel my hair and lean back to soak up some sun, enjoying the moment. Then my phone rings.

"Oh, yeah," Paige says, "it rang a couple of times."

I scramble, digging in my beach bag until I untangle my phone from a scarf, then look to see it's Fran. "Hi, Fran," I say cheerfully. "What's up?"

"Can you come back?" she asks in a hoarse voice.

"Sure."

She hangs up quickly, and I pretend to still be talking to her. Dumb, I know, but I want to avoid Paige's suspicion. "Sure, Fran, I can help with that. Paige and I just shot some beach stuff with JJ." I pause like I'm listening. "Yeah, I'll head on up there now."

"What's going on with Fran?" Paige tips up her sunglasses to peer curiously at me.

"She just wants me to go over some things for the show with her. Remember how I've been interning with her?"

"Oh." Paige nods. "I'll head up in about twenty minutes. I'm going to shower and change, and then we can go shopping and get a late lunch. Okay?"

"Sounds great." I gather my stuff, shove my feet into my sandals, and casually walk toward the hotel, but as soon as I'm out of Paige's sight, I begin to run. For some reason I have a feeling that Fran is really sick. Like maybe she needs to go to the hospital.

I knock on her door, and when she doesn't answer I let myself into my room and use the adjoining door. "Fran?" I call when I see that she's not in her bed, or even in the room.

"In here," she answers in a weak voice.

I go into the bathroom to see her lying on the white marble floor. Blood is splattered everywhere. "Fran!" I cry as I get on my knees next to her. "What happened? Did you cut yourself?"

"I was vomiting ... and I didn't make it to the toilet ... and then I fell down."

"But this blood—" I stop myself when I see a drop of blood trickle down the side of her mouth. "Were you vomiting blood?"

She nods with tears in her eyes. "It's normal, Erin. Just ulcerated bleeding ... from all the meds ... if you could get some Pepto-Bismol ... I think it would help."

"First let's get you cleaned up," I say as I help her to her feet then get her to sit on the lid of the toilet. I carefully remove her blood-splattered T-shirt, putting a bathrobe around her shoulders while I find a set of sweats I'd unpacked yesterday. Then I help her to get dressed and walk back to bed. "I'll put a wastebasket by your bed just in case you need to throw up again. No more running to the bathroom. Okay?"

She nods and leans back into her pillow. "Thank you."

I study her closely. "About the blood, Fran, maybe I should call a doctor and—"

"It's happened before," she says quietly but firmly. "This too will pass ..." She sighs and closes her eyes. "Just need time. And Pepto-Bismol."

"I'm going to run down to the hotel shop." I pause at the door, picking up the little hanging sign. "Maybe I should put this do not disturb sign on your door in case the maids try to come in."

"Yes. I don't want them to see that ... bathroom."

"Right." I suspect this means I'll get to clean it up. As I'm going down the elevator, I can feel my adrenaline pumping. This thing with Fran is so stressful. When I saw her all bloody like that, I was sure she was dying. Maybe she *is* dying. Can I really trust her—that this is normal? How would I even know?

Fortunately, the gift store in the hotel has Pepto-Bismol. I also get some Tums and a couple of cartons of yogurt too. As I'm taking these to the elevator, I run into Paige coming in from the beach.

"What's in the bag?" she asks as we ride up.

"Something for Fran," I admit. "She's got a stomachache."

"Too bad." Then she steps away from me with wide eyes. "I hope it's not catching."

"Me too. Just in case, you'd better keep your distance from her today." What we'll all do tomorrow is a mystery.

"Tell her to get well," Paige says as we part ways.

If only it were that simple, I think as I go through my room and into Fran's. "Paige said to get well," I announce a bit glibly as I close the door.

"What?" Fran looks alarmed. "Did you tell her?"

"She thinks you have the flu."

"Oh."

After a dose of Pepto-Bismol, I get Fran to eat some yogurt. Then I offer to go over tomorrow's plan with her. I'm surprised at how intricate it is; she almost has every minute scheduled. And the detailed schedule continues throughout the week: the various fashion shows, the *Britain's Got Style* show, and so on. It's all laid out like a well-formulated battle plan, and I can tell that if we don't stick to it, there will be problems. "We have quite a week," I say to her as I close her laptop. "You think you're going to be able to do this?"

"I don't know."

I'm trying to remember how many times she's said that— *I don't know, I don't know.* If Fran doesn't know, who does?

"While you were downstairs, I recalled that something like this happened quite a bit the other time."

"Huh?"

"Vomiting blood," she says quietly. "My stomach got really irritated before. Then I got better. And your yogurt and Pepto-Bismol seemed to help." She makes a weak smile. "If you decide to give up TV, you might consider taking up medicine."

Or housekeeping, I think as I go into the disaster-area bathroom and attempt to clean most of the mess up with tissues. Finally I resort to a wet towel. Using it like a mop, I manage to make the bathroom look somewhat respectable again. I'm just finishing up when I hear my phone ringing. I run to get it and see that it's Paige.

"You ready to go shopping?"

I glance over to where Fran is resting in bed. She seems okay right now, but who knows what's next? And what if she needs me and I'm at some store? "I think I should stay with Fran," I tell Paige.

"Really? Is she *that* sick?"

"Well, she threw up."

"Ugh."

"So, if you don't mind, maybe you could just head out on your own." I glance at Fran and see she's relieved.

"But I really wanted you with me, Erin. It's no fun to go shopping alone."

"Take JJ," I suggest. "In fact, you should take him so he can film you while you explore the island." Fran nods as if this is a good idea.

"It would be better if you were along too. One girl shopping alone is kind of bleak ... and a little pathetic, don't you think?"

"I have a feeling you can spark it up if you try, Paige."

"Maybe. But it won't be fun. Now it'll feel more like work."

"I know. And I'm sorry. You know as well as I do, if Fran doesn't get to feeling better, we'll have a hard time doing the show this week."

"You're right."

After I hang up, I look at Fran and see that her eyes are closed. Whether she's actually sleeping or just playing possum is anyone's guess. I straighten her room a bit, since I doubt that we'll be getting maid service in here, and go into my room, leaving the door open between us. I fire up my computer and start reading about leukemia.

It's not the first time I've researched this. I like information and I always hope that if you look long and hard enough, you can find the answer to just about anything. Unfortunately, leukemia could be the exception to this rule, because no matter how much I look, there doesn't seem to be any rock-solid answers. And, of course, there is no certain cure. Sometimes treatment works on the kind of leukemia Fran has, but most of the time, it doesn't.

Finally, I decide to call Mom. She's back from Paris and answers her cell phone from Jon's place. *Her* new place, I remember.

"Erin," she says happily. "How are you, sweetheart?"

I exchange a few pleasantries, inquire about their Paris trip, and then I go into my bathroom, just in case Fran can hear me, close the door, and give her a long update about Fran's condition.

"Oh, dear, Erin. That sounds serious."

"That's what I thought too. I wonder if she should go to a hospital."

"That's a good question."

"My biggest question is, should I tell Helen about this?"

"I wish Fran had told her."

"Me too."

"Well, it's Sunday. I suppose you could call Helen at home."

"Or I could wait and see if Fran really does get better by tomorrow. She keeps thinking she's going to turn a corner. I've seen her go through chemo treatments before, and she'll be so wiped out I think she's going to die, and the next thing I know she's up and dressed and ready to go."

"What's on the docket for tomorrow?" Mom asks. "Is it a very full day?"

I tell her about the swimsuit shoot on the beach and a fashion show we'll catch in the afternoon. "It's not jam-packed, but it's busy. Although I suppose I can try to cover for Fran if she's dragging. I wish Leah had been able to come with us."

"Maybe you should call Helen tomorrow and ask her to send Leah," Mom says. "Tell her Fran is ill and needs some extra assistance. You don't have to tell Helen everything. Just that you're a little short-handed. She should understand."

"You're right."

"I'm sorry you got stuck in the middle of that whole mess," Mom says. "It really doesn't seem fair. That's a lot for Fran to put on you."

"Well, Fran's got a lot weighing on her too."

"I know. And you feel free to call me for anything, Erin. Even if it's just to unload. Okay?"

"Thanks, Mom."

I do feel a little better after I hang up. I think Mom is right. This can probably wait until tomorrow. Helen will be in her office then, and hopefully she can send Leah out on the next plane. In the meantime, I'll continue to pray. But I'm starting to wonder — where is that miracle I've been asking for?

Chapter
13

On Monday I feel hopeful. By the time I check on her, Fran is up and dressed and assuring me she's over the hump and ready for the day.

"Did you eat anything?" I ask, feeling like her mother.

She points to a tray of partially eaten food. "And I had the other yogurt you brought me last night."

Satisfied that we might pull this off, I go to Paige's suite, where Shauna and Luis are already set up for hair and makeup, and where Paige is selecting today's wardrobe for us.

"I was reading about new designers who are debuting here this week," she calls over to me from the closet. "Remember Rhiannon Farley?"

"Yes," I say eagerly. "In New York. I loved her designs."

"Well, it says here that she's partnering with Eliza Wilton to—"

"Rhiannon is partnering with *Eliza*?" I turn my head, causing the eyeliner Shauna was applying to go across my nose.

"Nice move," she says as she reaches for a tissue.

"Sorry." I turn back around. "That is stunning news, Paige. Are you sure you read it right?"

"Yes. Apparently Eliza is the financial backing and business part of the deal and, naturally, Rhiannon brings the creativity."

"That's crazy. I can't imagine two more different people."

Paige laughs. "Kind of like you and me?"

"I guess."

"But remember, Rhiannon and Eliza went to school together with Taylor and DJ and those other girls that Katherine Carter was grooming for the fashion world."

I smile to myself as I recall DJ's recounting of her grandmother's high aspirations for those "Carter house girls." Maybe the old woman had some influence after all. Especially since three of the girls are making a splash in the fashion scene. "So does that mean Rhiannon is here in the Bahamas?" I ask Paige.

"Yes, and it looks like she's showing some casual wear during the same time slot as the *Couture* show tomorrow morning, which we're scheduled to cover. It says here that Rhiannon is part of the Eco Show."

"So we'll miss Rhiannon's show?"

"Unfortunately."

"What if we split up?" I suggest. "I could take my camera to Rhiannon's show and get some —"

"I don't know." Paige sounds doubtful. "You'd better check with Fran."

"Right."

So as soon as I'm done in hair and makeup, I hurry back to Fran's room, where she is on the phone and the computer and looking almost like her normal self. I wait for her phone conversation to end then pitch my new idea.

"I want to cover part of the Eco Show," I tell her. "I thought I could take my camera over there tomorrow, while you guys are shooting the *Couture* show."

Fran frowns, looking as if she's about to nix my idea. Suddenly she shrugs. "Okay."

"Okay?" I nod eagerly. "I can do that?"

"I actually think it's a good idea. Maybe you should set up some interviews with some of the other eco designers too."

"Really?"

"It's a good opportunity, Erin."

"So I can take one of the camera guys with me?"

She grabs a copy of our schedule and begins highlighting certain things in yellow. "These are the events you must attend with Paige. Anything you can fit in between these times is up for grabs." She then highlights some other things in pink. "These are some of the events where I think we can get by with one cameraman. I want to keep JJ and the rest of the crew with Paige, but if you want to take Alistair with you, I'm okay with it." She gives me the schedule as well as a printout list of designers and contact numbers.

I can't believe how relaxed Fran is about all this. She's usually much more of a control freak. Then I remember what she's dealing with, and the realization is bittersweet.

The first thing on today's docket is the swimsuit shoot. I'd heard that the most beautiful bodies are to be seen at Bahamas Fashion Week, and now I know that it's true. And they are not all stick-thin emaciated either. Many of the models look fairly healthy and robust, as if they work out. Both men and women come here from all different countries, and they are overwhelmingly gorgeous. To see them posing against the golden sand and turquoise water is spectacular.

Unfortunately, the weather is being less than cooperative. The wind is gusting, which knocks down one of the changing tents, and the rapid cloud movement plays havoc with the crew's lighting. It all makes for some interesting moments and fun footage, and our cameramen seem to be enjoying themselves.

As we work on this shoot, in between times when Paige and I are actually doing our commentary, I'm sneaking peeks at the list of eco designers and making some phone calls. By the time we wrap it up, I have a Haitian designer willing to be interviewed at twelve thirty this afternoon.

"I've got Murielle Leconte set for an interview," I tell Fran. "I'll do it while Paige is meeting with Andrew Harris."

Fran blinks rapidly. "Really? That's great." Then she tells me that since the Andrew Harris interview is in our hotel, Alistair and I can take the rental van to where the Leconte group is set up.

On the way to Murielle's hotel I quickly peruse a website I found that has some photos of her designs. She uses bright, island-friendly colors and natural materials, and everything has a happy, light feeling. I mentally compare her clothes to the designs that Brogan Braxton put together—and while they both utilize bright colors, Brogan's pieces seemed flat, with no flare or personality. They reminded me of paint-by-number, whereas Murielle's designs feel alive and active and real—more like original works of art.

·As it turns out, I need a translator to interview Murielle. As a result, I keep my questions very basic and general and then focus much of the time and camera on her designs. She not only designs beautiful clothing, but also bags, scarves, household items, and jewelry. She uses a lot of burlap, a design twist that I love, and the texture makes a great contrast with the bright colors. When we finish, I feel that despite the language barrier, we are *simpatico*. I thank her profusely and she gives me one of her wonderful burlap bags.

"Well done," Alistair tells me as we drive back to the hotel. "Although I'm surprised Fran let you do it."

"Yeah, I'm a little surprised too. At least we're getting extra footage for the show. I'm hoping to get enough for a whole episode on eco design."

"That's a great idea."

We make it back in time for the Peter Nygård casual wear show, where Paige is already doing her thing. Alistair and I join her as we get some on-the-spot interviews and shots of models. Then Paige and I find our seats and the show begins. But as the models start working the runway, I realize I haven't seen Fran around. I know she likes to stay behind the scenes, but I can usually spot her.

"Where's Fran?" I ask Paige as a model wearing a striped, hooded dress struts by.

"I thought she was with you."

"Oh." I simply nod, as if that makes sense. But now I'm wondering *where is Fran?* And is she okay?

After the show, Paige snags a few words with Peter. Then we pack it up and head back to the hotel to order some dinner and get ready for tonight's big event — local and renowned designer Kevin Evans is showing evening wear.

"Did you find out what happened to Fran?" Paige asks as we ride back to the hotel.

"I'm not sure. Maybe she's still sick."

"Well, we should probably call Helen." Paige lets out an exasperated sigh. "Because there's no way we can keep this machinery rolling without our director. Maybe Helen can send Leah out here to help."

"That's probably a good idea." I feel a mixture of relief and panic now. Relieved that Leah will be here to help us. Panicked that Fran's "secret" will soon be exposed and she could lose her job. But, really, what can I do?

"Dylan should be arriving in Nassau about now," Paige says happily as we go through the hotel lobby. "His show's not scheduled until Thursday, but he's coming early to check out the competition."

"And to spend time with you?"

"Absolutely!"

"Where's he staying?" I ask.

"In our hotel, *of course*."

"Right . . ."

"After the Evans show tonight, Dylan and I are attending the after party at Balmoral Club," Paige announces as we emerge from the elevator. "You can come along if you want."

"Thanks, but I think I'll pass."

Paige doesn't seem to care.

I check our schedule. "So I guess we have a couple hours before the next show."

"Yes. I'm going to take a shower and order some dinner," she tells me. "Shauna and Luis should be here around six-ish. Come on over whenever you're ready."

I agree to this and hurry into my room then on through the adjoining door, where I find Fran in her bed, looking like death warmed over.

"How's it going?" I ask, trying to mask the concern I feel.

"Not so well."

"What are we going to do?" I ask gently.

She closes her eyes and shakes her head.

"I think I need to call Helen," I say firmly.

"I know ..." She looks up at me with tears in her eyes. "I never should've come here, Erin. It was selfish."

I don't know how to respond to that. I do understand ... partially. But, yes, it was selfish. She's put both our show and her health at risk.

"I just wanted to get beyond"—she weakly waves her hands over the messy bed—"*this*. I just wanted to be well."

"That's what I wanted too, Fran. But it doesn't seem to be happening."

I return to my room to call Helen, but when I get her voicemail, I'm not sure how much to say. I hate sounding like a tattletale. And, really, Fran should be the one to tell Helen the whole truth. So I simply ask Helen to return my call as soon as possible. Then I call Mom and spill the whole story.

"I'm coming," she says abruptly.

"Huh?"

"I'm going to get on a plane and fly out there ASAP."

"*What?*" I collapse in the chair by the window and stare out over the beautiful tropical scene, trying to process what my mom is saying.

"I'm a director, Erin. You girls need one."

"Yes, but—"

"You girls are in a tight spot and I'm coming to help out. I'm sure Helen won't mind. Remember, she offered me the job once. Even so, I'll call her and straighten this whole thing out before I leave."

"But what about your job? And Jon?"

She laughs. "Jon will understand. And my job ... Well, I have a feeling that I've been replaced already anyway."

"What?"

"I'll explain it all when I get there, Erin. Right now I want to see if I can get a flight out of here tonight. That way I'll be in the Bahamas by morning and we'll all be ready to hit the road running."

"Seriously?" I'm about to cry, I'm so happy. "You can really do that?"

"I can and, unless there's a problem getting a flight, I will. In the meantime, why don't you email me anything I can start going over on the flight. Your schedule for the next few days, a list of your crew and responsibilities, that sort of thing. Can you do that?"

"Absolutely."

"I'll download the Fashion Week schedule so I can be on top of that too."

I can't believe it when it I hang up. It's like my mom suddenly turned into Superman. Or Supermom. Anyway, I'm so happy to think Mom's on her way that I run over to Paige's suite and spill the good news.

"What?" Paige cinches the belt of her bathrobe more tightly around her waist, frowning at me as if she's not heard me correctly.

So I explain more slowly. But Paige is scowling now. She is definitely not as pleased as I am about this rescue plan.

"What's wrong?" I ask.

"I cannot believe you went and did that, Erin. *Behind my back?*"

"Behind your back?"

"Yes. I'm part of this show. A pretty big part, as a matter of fact. But you sneak off and ask Mom to come out here to direct for us without even consulting me?"

"I thought you'd be glad to—"

"What about Helen? Did she agree to this?"

"Helen didn't answer her phone and I called Mom to—"

"Just because Fran's got a little bug, you can't go around hiring someone to replace her, Erin. You're not in charge of this show and you're not—"

"I know I'm not in charge," I say loudly. "But Fran has got more than a little bug, Paige." I'm angry now. And tired of playing games. In fact, I'm very close to telling Paige everything about Fran's leukemia, but I know this is not the right time. "We need a director to get through the next few days. Mom is dropping everything to get here and—"

"What about Mom's job?"

"She didn't seem worried. She's trying to get a red-eye flight tonight, and plans to be here by morning."

Paige twists her mouth in the same way she used to as a child, just before she'd stamp her foot. At least she's moved past that now.

"Why are you so upset about this anyway?" I demand. "I thought it was great of Mom to do this for us. It's a real lifeline."

"Yes, it's great, Erin. Just great." She lets out an exasperated sigh as she picks up her iPhone, checking it for messages.

A little light goes on inside my head. "Is this about Dylan?" I ask her. "I mean *you and Dylan*?"

Paige shakes her head then stomps off to her bathroom, slamming the door loudly. I know I hit the nail right smack on the head. Paige *is* worried. She's afraid that having Mom here is going to upset her romantic plans. She wants to be free to do as she pleases with her fiancée, and she's concerned that her mother could put a damper on everything. Well, get over it, sister!

Chapter
14

The Evans show is a big one, and I think it might be my favorite yet. The music is totally Caribbean, the colors and styles quintessential Bahamas. The general feel is very upbeat, fun, and carefree.

Afterward, as Paige gets a few words from Kevin and some of the models, we spot Taylor, Eliza, and Rhiannon. With cameras still running, we enjoy a happy little reunion and find out all of them are heading off to the after party.

"You're both coming too, aren't you?" Taylor asks. As usual, the girl looks stunning, but even more so in a tropical print halter dress from the show she modeled for. Combined with her dark wavy hair and caramel-colored skin, she looks like she belongs here.

"Dylan should be here soon to pick me up." Paige smiles as she peers through the crowd, no doubt hoping to spot him.

"By the way, congratulations," Taylor tells her. "Dylan has been one happy camper since you two got engaged."

"We were a little shocked," Eliza says in a stiff voice. "I thought you and Benjamin Kross were still together." She straightens a thin strap of her stark white sundress and I can't help but notice that her spray-on tan, while good, doesn't look quite as natural as my sister's.

"That was what the media wanted everyone to think," Paige replies lightly. "Fortunately, they were wrong."

"Right ..." Eliza nods, but her expression looks dubious. I remember that Eliza had her eyes on Dylan too. Hopefully she can set aside her jealousy now that Paige and Dylan are officially engaged.

"I'm coming to your show tomorrow," I tell Rhiannon, partly to change our conversation's focus and partly because I'm excited I get to cover it. I explain about how Paige and I are splitting up to cover more fashion.

"It's going to be a really small show," Rhiannon explains. "I'm sharing it with several other new designers."

"Small or not, at least you're here and showing," I tell her. "Kudos to you."

She smiles at Eliza. "It's thanks to Eliza," she says.

"Yes, we read about that," Paige says to them. "Sounds like a nice little partnership."

"It was actually Taylor's idea," Rhiannon says.

"But I was happy to get involved," Eliza says quickly. "I'm moving on from modeling, but I want to remain in the fashion world." She smiles at Rhiannon. "And I believe in this little girl and her designs."

The camera crew is shutting down now, and JJ comes right over to Taylor and her eyes light up. It seems the two of them are picking up right where they left off in France. "So is everyone heading to the after party?" Taylor asks again.

"Not me," I admit.

"Why not?" Rhiannon asks. "It's supposed to be great."

"Oh, our director is under the weather and I thought I'd check on her."

"Just give her a call," Eliza suggests.

I consider this, but if she's sleeping, the phone will disturb her, and if she's feeling really bad, she probably won't even answer. Suddenly I feel resentful of how I'm stuck playing nursemaid to Fran. Really, she is supposed to be taking care of *us*.

"Come on," Paige urges me. "Fran's probably asleep anyway."

"Maybe I could go for just a little while," I agree.

But "a little while" ends up being until after midnight. Still, the music is so good—a real Calypso band. And the food—an island banquet—is abundant and delicious. And it's so fun to visit with both old and new friends ... it's hard to leave. But I know I must.

Although everyone else stays at the party, which is in full swing, I call a taxi and return to the hotel feeling a bit like Cinderella. When I tiptoe in to check on Fran, she seems to be sleeping comfortably. I realize I probably could've stayed at the party after all.

My phone rings before seven in the morning, but when I groggily answer, I'm pleased to hear Mom's voice. "Our plane just touched down," she tells me. "I'll be at your hotel in less than an hour."

I tell her my room number and, feeling a great sense of relief, pull on some sweats and start making coffee. Before long Mom and I are hugging.

"I don't think Paige is awake yet," I say as I hand her a cup of coffee.

"I didn't expect she would be."

I order us some breakfast, and Fran's as well. While we wait, we have our coffee on the terrace, enjoying the fresh morning air and the view.

"Ah, paradise." Mom smiles happily.

"It really is beautiful." I look out to where the palm trees are swaying in the breeze, the ocean is varying shades of turquoise and sapphire, and a few white clouds interrupt the clear blue sky as they wisp along. So peaceful ... especially in the morning.

"You'd never suspect there's a hurricane's brewing out there in the Atlantic."

"Really?" I stare out at the serene scene.

"I saw it on the news at LAX last night. You hadn't heard?"

"No. I haven't really been paying attention to the news. Is it supposed to come near here?"

"I think there's a slim chance, but you know how those things go. You never can tell."

"I haven't heard a word about it." I frown.

"Probably because it's unlikely it'll actually develop into anything serious. That's pretty rare this time of year."

"Even so, it would sure put a damper on some of these fashion shows. You'd think someone might've mentioned it."

"I'm guessing Fran hasn't heard anything either." Mom takes a sip of coffee. "How is she anyway?"

"I haven't checked on her yet this morning." I glance inside my room, to the adjoining door I left partially open. "She was pretty bad yesterday. Maybe I should check on her."

"Maybe so."

As I head to Fran's room, I realize she has no idea my mom is coming, or is in fact here now. I wonder how I'll break this to her. But when I see her, still in bed and looking just as worn out as yesterday, I have a feeling she won't care. Maybe she'll even be relieved.

"How are you feeling?" I ask quietly.

She sighs. "About the same."

"I tried to call Helen," I tell her. "Anyway, I left a message."

"Did you tell her about me?"

"No . . . I just asked her to call back."

"Did she?" Fran's eyes seem almost fearful, like she sees everything coming to a quick, unhappy ending.

I explain about my mom being here and how she'll step in as director, if that's okay with Fran.

Fran blinks. "Well, I guess I have no choice."

"Maybe if you rest and eat the right things . . . maybe you'll perk up in a few days. You know, like you were doing before."

"Maybe." Her brow creases with doubt.

"Anyway, I ordered you some breakfast." I move around the room, straightening here and there. "And if you don't mind, I'd like to make sure you get some housekeeping service today. Even if you have to be here while the maid comes in."

"Yes . . . that's okay . . . I don't expect you to do my house-keeping." There's a bitter edge to her voice, and I try not to feel resentful as I heat up some water for her tea.

"My mom says there's a hurricane coming."

"Coming here?"

"Well, that's hard to say. But apparently it's out there."

"Give me the remote," she commands.

I hand her the remote, and while she's jumping from channel to channel I make her a cup of green tea, adding just a little sugar the way she likes it. I also set her box of crackers by her bed. "Try to get something in your stomach," I tell her, "until breakfast gets here."

"There it is," she tells me, pointing to the Weather Channel. "Hurricane Bruce is missing Haiti and passing along Turks and Caicos today."

"Meaning?"

"If it stays on course, it might pass us by."

"It might?"

She picks up her tea. "Or it might not."

"You probably already feel like you've been hit by a hurricane."

She barely nods. "Hurricane Leukemia."

"I was reading online about bone marrow transplants," I tell her. "It sounded pretty hopeful."

She sets down her tea with a thud. "Yes—hopeful for those who find a match."

"So have you been looking?"

"Oh, sure, my doctor has me registered. If a match ever comes through ... if I last long enough ... I might get a chance."

"I was thinking that maybe I should register," I say quietly.

She gives me a half smile. "You think you'd be my match?"

"No ... I mean, I doubt it. But I might be able to help someone."

She closes her eyes and leans back. "I'm so tired ... Erin ... so tired."

I take the hint and leave her to rest. When I get back to my room, Mom isn't there. I check the bathroom, and she's not there either. Then I hear loud voices in the room next to mine—Paige's room. As I press my ear to the wall, I can hear that it's Mom and Paige and Dylan—and it doesn't sound good.

"Well, I certainly didn't expect that," Mom says as she comes back into the room.

"Was Dylan there?" I ask cautiously.

She nods and sits down, crossing one leg over the other and pressing her lips tightly together.

"He spent the night?" I say quietly.

She nods again, then shakes her head. "I am so ashamed."

"*Ashamed?*" I try to grasp this. "Of Paige?"

"Of myself."

"Oh ...?" I wonder if she thinks she's been a negligent mother. And maybe she has been distracted, but to be fair, Paige and I are both over eighteen.

"I'm ashamed that I'm acting like my mother."

"Huh?"

"I just laid into Paige and Dylan, treating them like errant children." She covers her face with her hands. "I'm so embarrassed."

Okay, now I'm really confused. "*You're* embarrassed?"

"Yes. It was very immature on my part."

"Why?"

She looks at me in surprise. "Why?"

"Yes. Why? I mean, they're not married yet."

"Well, yes ... but they *are* engaged, Erin."

"I know. But what about waiting for the wedding?"

She looks confused. "I suppose that's what I hoped they would do. But I realize that's not the way people are nowadays."

"Why not?" I demand. "Whatever happened to saving yourself for marriage?"

"I know you take abstinence seriously, Erin. I really respect that. But Paige is different. I need to respect that too."

Fortunately, room service arrives. I honestly don't know what I would've said if we'd continued this conversation. It's not exactly like a double standard, but something about this conversation feels whacked to me. And, once again, I feel like the odd woman out.

Chapter
15

For a variety of reasons, I'm extremely relieved to part ways with Paige, Mom, and the crew. Despite my opinion, which is quite outnumbered, Mom apologized to Paige and Dylan. I'm trying to get over it, but I still feel like I must've been born in the wrong generation, or about a hundred years too late. Consequently, I'm very quiet as Alistair drives us over to the Eco Show.

"Everything okay with you?" he asks in a slightly concerned tone.

"Yeah. Sorry, I guess I was just thinking." I glance over my notes.

"It's cool that your mom could come out and help with the show."

"I think Fran appreciates it."

"How's Fran doing?" he asks as he turns toward the hotel that's hosting the Eco Show.

"I think she'll be better with some rest."

"Tell her I'm thinking of her."

"I will." I change the subject as he pulls into the line of

traffic snaking toward the entrance. "So did you hear about the hurricane?"

"Yeah, but it sounds like it's going to miss this island."

"I'm sure that will make a lot of people happy." I start to gather my things as he pulls under the portico. He tells me he'll catch up with me inside.

My plan is to stay as busy as possible in the Bahamas from now on. I will escape the confusion of my family's personal problems, as well as Fran's health challenges, by losing myself in the show. It seems a sensible plan. As a matter of fact, I realize now that all this busyness has helped me escape from my own personal life as well. I have barely thought twice about Blake. And, for now, that's how I'd like to keep it. Like my mom said, work can be therapeutic. And in my case, it's more like a path to amnesia.

I start by interviewing Rhiannon, who is like a breath of fresh air in this crazy fashion world. Like me, she's a Christian who tries to mesh her beliefs into her work.

"I believe God gave me a gift of creativity," she says to me about midway through the interview. "As well as a love of fashion. At first I was uncertain about the whole thing. I thought maybe it was wrong for a Christian to be involved in the fashion industry."

"And why is that?" I ask.

"The fashion industry has a reputation." She smiles.

"A reputation for what?"

"Oh, you know. Drugs, money, warped values ... body image problems. The works."

"So how do you reconcile that?" I ask.

"Well, I realized that those issues are everywhere. And, yes, they're present in this industry too. But I thought maybe if I brought my creativity into the industry, maybe if I brought my beliefs ... you know." She shrugs. "Maybe I can make a difference. Even if it's in a small way."

"I think you're making a difference," I tell her. "Maybe in a big way too. And speaking of differences, tell me a bit about your philosophy for green design. We know you're a participant in the Eco Show. Can you share with our viewers why designing green clothes is important to you?"

"To start with, I was brought up in a fairly impoverished home. So I learned early on to make do with whatever was at hand. I also learned to sew. If I needed an outfit for an event, I would sometimes take something from my mom's closet and rework it into something different. Or else I would hit the local thrift stores. So reusing and recycling comes naturally to me. I thrive on vintage. In high school I lived with several girls—"

"Is this the house you lived in with Katherine Carter, former editor of *Couture* magazine?"

"Yes. Mrs. Carter graciously allowed me to live in her home for free. In fact, she is one of the major reasons I am where I am today. It was quite a challenge living with a bunch of rich girls." Her eyes twinkle as she smiles. "I tried hard to keep up in regard to fashion. That's when I really had to gather lots of retro and vintage clothes and fabrics and accessories, reworking them into something fresh and new. It wasn't long before I started designing for some of my friends."

"Including renowned model Taylor Mitchell?" I ask.

"That's right. As well as my new business partner, Eliza Wilton, who recently retired from modeling."

We talk awhile longer, but because Rhiannon still has last-minute preparations to attend to, we end it. "We'll be getting footage of your show," I promise. "And if you don't mind, I'll do some behind-the-scenes shots too."

"Of course I don't mind." She beams. "Being on your show is fantastic. Thanks so much for thinking of me."

"And thank you for what you contribute to the fashion industry, Rhiannon." I wave at Alistair now. "Seriously," I say quietly to her as soon as Alistair's camera is down. "I'm so glad you're doing what you're doing. It's easy to feel jaded in this industry."

She gets a thoughtful look. "You know ... whenever I feel jaded or negative about something, I try to remember to ask myself: *What am I looking at?*" She reaches out and squeezes my hand. "Because I never feel jaded when my eyes are on God, Erin."

"Wow, that's good to remember. Thanks."

"So are you coming to the Eco Show's after party tonight?" Rhiannon asks.

"I, uh, I don't know. I mean, I wasn't invited or—"

"Come with me," she says suddenly. "Be my guest. Eliza's going to a different party. One of the British designers is having a big shindig. But I want to do the eco party. It's more my style."

"I'd love to go, but I should check with my sister first."

"Sure. I'm guessing she'll be at the other one. Call me if you decide you want to come. It might be easier just to meet there."

I thank her again and wish her good luck, and then Alistair and I do a quick interview with Eliza, which Rhiannon suggested. As I hear Eliza talking about the business end of things, I'm impressed that she's quite knowledgeable. I think maybe she and Rhiannon make a good pair despite their obvious differences. After this ends, I find my seat near the runway while Alistair takes a spot on the sidelines with the other photographers.

Rhiannon's show is short but delightful. Her line of clothes is light and breezy, fairy-like in an island sort of way. She utilizes some soft, natural fibers, colored with vegetable dyes. Her look is very different from the other designers, but it's romantic and feminine and sweetly appealing. I have a feeling I'm not the only one who appreciates her unique designs, because the audience is as enthusiastic as I am.

After the show, I wish I had more time to talk to Rhiannon, but probably not as much about fashion as philosophy, because her words about God are still ringing in my ears. Anyway, she seems to have her hands full and I need to move on, since I managed to get Eric Raisina, an eco designer from Madagascar, to talk to me before his show.

Alistair and I hurry to where Eric is putting the finishing touches on his models. In the midst of the usual behind-the-scenes chaos, I ask him a few questions while Alistair gets some footage. Then I sit in on his show while Alistair films. It's another amazing production, with incredible drumming music, fantastic colors, and it's just plain fun. In my follow-up comments I praise Eric, and his homeland, Madagascar, for producing such a brilliantly creative designer.

We film several others, including BoUik from Jamaica, which turns out to be another high-energy, colorful show. To my surprise it's after eight o'clock by the time Alistair and I are packing it up and heading for the van. We're tired, but I think we got some good material.

I check my phone as Alistair drives us back to the hotel and am surprised to see that both Paige and Mom have called me several times. I've had my phone on silent mode, and this is the first time I've checked it since early this afternoon. I listen to the first message, and it's Paige sounding frantic because Alistair and I aren't at the Taylor-Hasana show.

"Uh oh," I say to Alistair. "Sounds like we're in trouble."

"What's up?"

I listen to the next message, which is nearly identical to the first one. The other messages are also pretty much the same. When I tell Alistair that we missed the Taylor-Hasana show, he lets out a low whistle.

"That was a big show, wasn't it?"

"Yeah. But they should've been able to handle it."

"It sure doesn't sound like it."

"Well, you've got to expect some bumps when you go from one director to another. Someone obviously dropped the ball."

"That's right," I agree. "And there are worse things than missing one fashion show, even if it was a big one."

Still, I'm a little worried as Alistair navigates the traffic to our hotel. I'm wondering if having my mom working as director might not be a bit of a challenge after all. Maybe Fran is feeling better. Of course, I know that if Fran is feeling better, she will be irked at me for missing the Taylor-Hasana show too, even though I didn't have it on my schedule. For some reason this designer from Granada is supposed to be really hot.

"That Eric Raisina show was really something, wasn't it?" Alistair says to me. He probably senses that I'm fretting over missing the other show.

"It was amazing," I admit. "But my favorite show of the day was still Rhiannon's. Of course, I'm probably biased toward her anyway. Still, I think that girl has a bright future, don't you?"

We make more fashion small talk, but the closer we get to the hotel, the more nervous I get. I have a feeling I'll not only have Mom and Paige on my case, but Fran as well. After Alistair drops me off and I'm pushing the elevator button to go up, I decide I don't really care. Let them fire me. It's not like I ever wanted to be part of this crazy ride in the first place. Fashion is *so* not my thing. And yet I was actually enjoying it today. It figures that as soon as I'm having a good time, I make everyone else mad.

As I ride up in the elevator, which is crowded with a bunch of ravenous models who are making dinner plans and barely even notice me, I recall Rhiannon's words about keeping her eyes on God. I realize that's some advice I need to put to use. So as the elevator stops on floor after floor, dropping off the hungry models, I lean against the back wall, close my eyes, and pray. First, being basically selfish, I ask God to sustain me through all this chaos and to let my light shine for him in an arena that seems fairly dark. Next, I ask for God to help Fran to get healthy and well. Then I ask God to help me be a better influence on my sister and mom—not that they seem to be paying much attention to me of late. Finally, I thank God for his promise to me—that no matter what, he will always be with me. I need that a lot just now.

When I get into my room I'm surprised to see that my mother has made herself at home and is already sound asleep in the king-sized bed. While I have no problem sharing accommodations with my mom, and I'm sure she's exhausted after her red-eye flight last night, I wonder why she doesn't room with Paige, since she's the one with the full suite. However, I think I know the answer to that question.

Seeing the light still on in Fran's room, I go over and

discover that she's sitting up in bed with her computer in her lap. "How are you doing?" I ask, quietly shutting the door behind me.

She shrugs, with her eyes still on the computer screen. "Okay."

"Are you working?"

"Just checking the weather."

"How's the hurricane doing?"

"Hovering."

"Huh?"

"Bruce can't seem to make up his mind." She closes her laptop then looks up at me. "So how was your day?"

I sit on the chair across from her and pour out my story of how fantastic the Eco Show was. "And you know what, Fran, I actually enjoyed the whole thing. These designers are truly refreshing with their new ideas and eco designs. I think Alistair and I got a lot of good footage. There could be two or three episodes out of what we filmed." I pause to catch my breath. "Of course, Helen might not want that many."

"Perhaps if they were interspersed with the others."

I nod eagerly. "And those episodes would appeal to a broader audience."

She makes a weary smile. "You're sounding a bit commercial."

I frown. "Well, isn't that how this works?"

"Yes. But it's different hearing it from you."

Now I feel frustrated, like no matter what I do, I'm wrong.

"I'm sorry, Erin." She sighs. "I didn't mean to rain on you."

"No, that's okay. I actually came back tonight thinking I was going to take some heat for missing the Taylor-Hasana show."

"Yes ... I heard about that."

"Are you mad at me too?"

She presses her lips together then shakes her head.

"And just so you know, I'm tracking with tomorrow's schedule. I know we've got the *Britain's Got Style* show and the rest of the agenda."

"Good ..." She pushes off the scarf that's wound around her head, setting it beside her. Her pale, bald head reminds me again of what she's actually dealing with.

I lean forward, peering intently at her. "So, really, how *are* you?"

She takes in a breath, slowly releasing it. "Not well."

"Not well ... as in worse?"

She nods, barely.

"You need to go home, Fran. You need to go to your doctor."

"You're probably right."

"That reminds me. Helen returned my call, and I explained how you were under the weather and that my mom came out to lend a hand."

"I know ..."

"Did Helen call you?"

"Yes ... after she spoke to you." Fran closes her eyes now and, pushing her laptop away from her, leans back into her pillows with a very tired sigh.

"You need to rest."

"Yes."

"We can figure this out in the morning."

All I hear now is the sound of her breathing, but it's not the relaxed, peaceful sound of someone resting comfortably. Instead it's a bit jagged and I can tell she's in pain. So I do something I've never done before. Not with her anyway. I begin to pray quietly, out loud. At first it feels extremely uncomfortable and slightly weird, but as I continue—pressing through the awkwardness—it becomes more natural. Or maybe it's supernatural. I ask God to heal her ... and help her ... and show her what she should do ... and to make the way for her to do it. Finally, I realize that her breathing sounds even and calm. She's asleep.

It's only a little past nine, but it feels like everyone has gone to bed. However, I realize that's probably only in these two rooms. The rest of the island is hopping and popping with after parties, dinners, and celebrations. I decide to take Rhiannon up on her invitation. I give her a call, and she sounds happy that I'm coming.

Of course, I realize that means I need to dress, and that means I need to go to Paige's room. I knock first, thinking there is no way she and Dylan would be in there this early in the evening. If they are, I will simply excuse my interruption, pick out an outfit, and leave as fast as possible. Fortunately, they aren't there.

So I go in and start picking through the dresses, finally settling on a Marc Jacobs number that's made of a filmy lavender fabric with ruffles. I choose it partly because it looks cool and comfortable and partly because it reminds me a bit of Rhiannon's designs. I pick out a pair of bronze metallic sandals and a little beaded evening bag by Michael Kors. I'm not sure what my sister would say, but I think I look fairly well put together. I touch up my makeup and hair then hurry down to the lobby and wait for a taxi.

As I'm waiting, I notice some models ahead of me in the taxi line. Two of them are consoling another one who's crying.

I try not to stare, but I am reminded—again—of how these beautiful young women who look so confident and perfect strutting down the runways are real people too. They have problems and challenges just like the rest of us. But unlike some of us, they have to cover these things up as they do their jobs. Otherwise they would be unemployed.

"Go ahead," the brunette girl tells me. "You can take that taxi. We need to sort this out first."

I thank them, flash a smile, and get into the taxi. As I think about those three beautiful women, I wonder—was I seeing them through God's eyes just now? Instead of my own?

Chapter

16

The after party for the Eco Show is being held on Paradise Island, and when the taxi drops me off, I can tell this is a pretty swanky party. Not that I expected it to be less. But I suppose, since these designers are so green and eco-friendly, I didn't expect it to be so *lavish*. Beautifully arranged tables hold an excess of gorgeous food, candles, and flowers. And everyone is dressed to the nines. I'm not sure what I thought this would be—maybe a beach party—but at least I'm dressed appropriately.

As I walk through the sprawling grounds, I call Rhiannon to tell her that I'm here. Before long we meet up, get some food, and find a table far enough from the Reggae band that we can hear each other.

"Your show was great," I tell her as I fork into a grilled prawn.

"Thanks, but compared to most of them, it was a small potato." She laughs. "But, hey, at least it was *my* potato."

We discuss some of the other eco shows and which ones we liked best and why. "Being at the eco shows makes me a lot more interested in fashion," I admit.

"Oh, that's right," she says. "You're the sister who's not that into it."

I nod as I take a bite. "But hearing what you said today is making me reconsider some things."

"What I said?" she looks puzzled.

"About trying to see things through God's eyes."

"Oh, yeah." She smiles. "Sorry, I'm a little fuzzy about our interview. I was so anxious about the show . . ."

"I totally understand."

"It's all gone by so fast." She stretches her neck and lets out what sounds like a relieved sigh. "But I'll be glad to go home."

"When do you leave?"

"Early tomorrow, which might be a good thing, considering the storm that's brewing out there. This is a great place to visit, but I don't think I'd want to be stuck here if Hurricane Bruce turned into a bad one."

"Do you think that's likely?"

"Eliza seems convinced that it's not going to hit here. She plans to stay on until next weekend. How about you?"

"We're staying until next Sunday too."

"I'm sure you'll be fine." She flashes her sunny smile.

"You really are an optimist, aren't you?" I tease.

"My friends still call me Pollyanna sometimes." Then she tells me a bit about her childhood, how her mother was a drug addict when she was young—how she went in and out of rehab, how she'd use their food money to buy drugs, and how she died from an overdose late last year. "To be honest, that was pretty tough. No one was calling me Pollyanna then."

"I'm so sorry," I say. "Now that you mention it, I remember hearing about that when we were in New York last winter."

"Anyway, my point is, living like that, I had to grow up fast. I was more like the parent with my mom. I was always über-worried about everything, always working, saving money, trying to make ends meet. It was really pretty pathetic."

"And yet you're such a positive person. How is that?"

"I didn't find God until I was fifteen. But it was so amazing, so real, so exactly what I needed—that I grabbed on tight and decided to put all my trust in him." She holds up her hands in a carefree way. "Basically ... I believe that God is my daddy and he takes very good care of me. So, really, I don't have anything to worry about, do I?"

"Your faith is a lot stronger than mine," I admit. I tell her about how my dad died and how maybe I'm still dealing with that on some levels. "It's like I'm afraid that everyone is going to leave or hurt me ... sooner or later." Then I tell her about how my mom just got married. "Jon is a great guy, but it feels like my mom has left me." Of course, then I have to explain how she actually just joined us here.

"That's so cool," Rhiannon says. "It must be fun."

"You'd think." I confess how I got on both my mom and sister's bad side today. "All because I stayed too long at the Eco Show."

She chuckles. "I'm sure you can iron that one out."

Now, since I seem to be baring my soul to this girl, I even tell her about how I'm struggling over Paige's relationship with Dylan. "Even my mom says I'm old-fashioned. I honestly don't know what to think anymore."

She nods in a thoughtful way. "You know, I went through some of that myself. It wasn't with a sister, but my friends at the Carter House were a lot like sisters. And some of them were making some pretty raunchy choices and doing things I totally did not agree with."

"So what did you do?"

"Sometimes I tried to talk to them, to tell them how I felt about what they were doing." She laughs. "Sometimes they called me Preacher Girl. Sometimes they listened. Eventually I came to realize that they were going to do what they were going to do and there was nothing I could do to stop them. Well, except for one thing." She holds a finger in the air. "I could pray."

"Right."

"I know, sometimes it doesn't sound like much, Erin. But I've kept on praying for them. And I've watched all those girls over the last few years, and I have to say their lives have changed in some cool ways. Oh, not everyone. Not yet anyway. But I feel hopeful."

I hang with Rhiannon, meeting her friends and socializing until after midnight. The party is still going strong, but she says she's going to call it a night. "Feel free to stay if you want," she finally tells me, "but my flight is early and I'm pretty exhausted. I think I'll head back to my hotel."

"I should too," I tell her. "We're doing *Britain's Got Style* tomorrow morning and if I'm not in top form, my sister will probably have my head on a platter."

We share a taxi and I wish her a good flight as she's dropped at her hotel. Then I check my phone for messages as I'm driven over to mine. Mostly I'm worried about Fran, and I'm relieved to see that there are no new messages. For me, at least for today, it seems that no news is good news. When I get to my room, I'm glad to see that both my mom and Fran seem to be sleeping soundly. As for my sister—and Dylan—I tell myself I don't care. But then, remembering Rhiannon's advice, I take it a step further and pray for both of them.

When I wake up in the morning, I can hear the sound of water rushing and I realize that it must be Mom taking a shower. I almost forgot she was here. It's only eight thirty, and I'm not too concerned since the schedule says we don't need to leave the hotel for our first gig, *Britain's Got Style*, until eleven.

I check on Fran, who is sitting up in bed watching the Weather Channel with worried eyes.

"What's the news?" I ask as I sit in the chair by her bed.

"Bruce appears to be heading our way."

"Really?" I peer curiously at the TV screen. "I've never been in a hurricane before. Should we be scared?"

She turns off the TV and looks at me. "I am scared."

"Oh?"

"Not of the hurricane — not exactly — but I am scared. I need to go home, Erin. As soon as possible."

"I know," I say eagerly. "That's what I've been trying to tell you."

"Can you book my flight?" she asks weakly. "Book it before Bruce gets here."

"When's that supposed to be?"

"They're predicting this afternoon."

"I'll do my best."

Then she tells me to get her purse and shows me which credit card to use.

"Do you think you'll be strong enough to fly?" I ask as I pull out the card.

"I have to be."

First I try to book a flight online, but there is nothing for today. So I decide to start calling airlines and, after long waits, I'm told the same. Today is booked solid. Apparently a lot of people are trying to get off the island before Bruce arrives, and it's standby only. "Bear in mind," one man warns me in a British accent, "if the hurricane does come this way, there will be no flights going or coming for some time."

Feeing a bit frantic, I go back to my room, where Fran can't hear me, and I try another tactic. "But I have someone here who is extremely ill," I tell a Delta person. "She needs to get home to see her doctor."

"Is this a medical transport?"

"I—uh—I don't know."

The woman gives me another number to call and, feeling a bit hopeless and a lot desperate, I try. This time I explain the situation in detail, and after a wait I'm told that even if we want to book this flight, it will be dependent on the weather.

"I understand," I tell her. "But I had hoped to get her out of here before the weather becomes a problem."

"It is already a problem."

"Oh."

"We could get an air ambulance to Nassau before the hurricane hits and, depending on the location of the hurricane at that time, we could possibly get out."

"Possibly?"

"I can't guarantee it," she says with exasperation. "I don't have a crystal ball. And I certainly can't control the weather."

"Right."

"This decision must be made quickly. And if you order an air ambulance from Miami to Nassau, you will be responsible for the bill whether or not you use our service."

"Even if the hurricane hits and she can't get out?"

"That's correct."

I ask her how much this service costs and nearly fall over when she gives me the quote. I'm pretty sure a family of four could fly around the globe for that price. "Can I call you back?"

"Of course, but every minute counts."

I'm just hanging up when my mom comes into the room, and her expression is not happy. "We have a problem," she tells me grimly.

"We have lots of problems," I say quickly. "And I don't have time for—"

"You'll have to make time, Erin."

"Look, if it's about yesterday, I'm sorry. I just got caught up—"

"No, no—this isn't about that. This is about Paige."

"Paige?"

Mom lets out a frustrated sigh. "She is seriously hungover."

"*Hungover?*"

"Yes. And we need to leave for *Britain's Got Style* in an hour and a half."

"So, tell Paige to get un-hungover," I say.

"I wish it were that simple." She shakes her head. "I think you'll have to handle it for her, Erin."

"Me?" I frown. "Handle what?"

"*Britain's Got Style.*"

I can't help but laugh. "Right. By myself? I'm no style critic. There's no way I can stand in for her."

"Well, there's no way she's going to make it. Right now she's in there throwing up."

"And what about Dylan in all this?" I demand. "Is he in

there throwing up too? Or did he simply contribute to the delinquency of a minor?"

"The legal drinking age is eighteen here, Erin."

For drama, I slap my forehead. "Oh, that's right. Maybe that's why they have Fashion Week here. Most of the models can be of legal drinking age."

"Point taken." Mom is pacing now. "And if it makes you feel better, Dylan is actually fairly contrite."

"I assume Dylan just sat by while Paige got totally wasted last night?"

"In her defense, they both said she didn't have that much to drink. It's just that she forgot to eat."

I ball my hands into fists and shake them in the air. "Isn't it bad enough that we've got Fran over there, practically dying—and not because she partied too hard either—and then Paige pulls a stunt like this?"

"How is Fran?"

I quickly explain what I know about the impending hurricane and how I'm trying to set up a medical transport to get her out of here.

"Isn't that terribly expensive?"

I nod. "Yes, as a matter of fact."

"Is the show covering it?"

"I have no idea, Mom. But I need to hurry and find out if Fran wants me to book it or not."

"Yes. Of course. Go and find out. I'll check on Paige again."

"And here's an idea," I toss at her as I'm halfway through the doorway. "Tell Dylan to take some responsibility for what happened with Paige. And maybe he'd like to replace her as a judge for *Britain's Got Style*."

Mom shakes her head. I hurry next door to find Fran with the Weather Channel on again, and I can tell by her expression that the news is not good. I quickly relay the information about the air ambulance and how we need to decide immediately. I mention what time it would get here and then drop the bombshell about how much it would cost. Her already pale face seems to get whiter.

"But this is the kicker," I say. "If the hurricane causes the air ambulance to be grounded in Nassau, you still have to pay. Even if they can't get you out."

"Seriously?"

"That's what she told me. I only spoke to one medical transport service. I don't know if they're all like that. The woman did say there's a possibility they can safely fly in and out—*if we move fast on this.*"

Fran points to the TV and shakes her head. "It's too iffy. The storm could be here by noon ... or later tonight."

"Or not at all," I offer.

"Yes ... or not at all." She waves her hand. "You need to go get ready for *Britain's Got Style.*" She looks at her clock. "Really, you should be in hair and makeup by now, Erin."

"Right ..." I turn and leave. No way am I going to tell her what a mess *that's* going to be. I head for Paige's room, but then I see Luis and Shauna coming down the hallway. I quickly give them the lowdown on the hangover.

"What are you going to do?" Shauna asks me as I knock on the door of Paige's room.

"I have no idea." When no one answers, I pull out the key card Paige gave me when we arrived, slide it through, and let us in. "Hello?" I call.

Dylan comes out of the bedroom with a guilty expression.

But Shauna and Luis simply greet him as if it's no big deal that he obviously slept here last night.

"Hey, Erin," he says to me, looking sheepish. "Your mom told me about your idea for me to replace Paige on the show. I'm sure no one would notice."

Luis thinks that's funny and he jokingly introduces the possibility of dressing Dylan up like Paige. "Dylan could probably make a big splash on their show."

"Hilarious," I say as Shauna points me to the makeup station. I frown at her. "I don't really see the point in getting me ready," I tell her as I sit down. "There's no way I can pull this off without Paige. We all know I'm no fashion expert."

"Well, at least you'll look nice for the day," Shauna says, using a sponge to blend foundation.

"I have an idea," Mom says as she emerges from the bedroom.

"How's Paige?" Luis asks with sympathy.

"Wiped out, but resting." Mom goes over to where Dylan is sitting by the window with a sad expression. She points at him. "It will require cooperation from you. Paige says your show's not until tomorrow. So you're probably not too busy today."

He shrugs. "Not too busy."

And just like that, like my mom thinks she's turned into a CIA agent, she starts describing a wild techie plan that is supposed to save the day. She wants me to wear a hidden earphone and for Dylan to be offstage watching the show via one of our cameras, which will be linked directly to his laptop. He will feed me fashion advice, direction, and critique.

"No way!" I shake my head, causing Shauna to jump back and scowl at me. "That is crazy."

"Why?" Luis asks. "It sounds like fun to me."

"That's because you don't have to do it," I tell him.

Dylan comes over to my chair. "I think we can pull it off."

"Seriously?" I frown at him. "But you wouldn't be the one on the hot seat, now would you?" I turn to Mom. "What happens if we lose our connection? Or if the *Britain's Got Style* people figure it out? And besides that, isn't it a little unethical?"

"We do that in the news all the time," Mom tells me. "Sometimes we need to get a message to the anchor while he's on the air and we can't always get it written out quickly enough. So we use—"

"But won't they see it?" I ask. "An earpiece?"

"I can cover it with your hair," Luis says quickly.

"And I can help conceal it on your neck," Shauna offers. "I've done things like that before."

"And you can wear big earrings and something with a collar," Mom suggests.

"This is crazy," I tell them, but they're already scrambling. Mom's on the phone with our crew, checking to see if they have the equipment. Dylan's on his computer trying to find out more about the British style show. Shauna leads me to the walk-in closet in the bedroom to find an appropriate outfit.

Meanwhile Paige looks a little green around the gills, curled up in a fetal position on the bed, groaning softly. I actually consider sniping something mean at her, but thankfully stop myself. Not only do I stop, but I feel slightly disgusted with myself. Especially in light of what Rhiannon told me last night. I can't believe how angry and judgmental I can be sometimes. A lot of times. Really, what is wrong with me?

So instead I go over and gently touch Paige's shoulder.

"I'm sorry you feel so lousy," I say quietly. "I hope you get to feeling better soon. I'll do what I can to rescue this."

"Thanks," she whispers.

Okay, I know that's a small step for most people, but in light of knowing how Paige got in this position and in light of the position she's put me in, it's a giant step for me.

Chapter
17

We arrive at the hotel where the show is being recorded this week and, to my relief, Mom is up front with the producer of *Britain's Got Style*. Without going into too much detail, she explains that Paige suddenly became ill and that because I'm not used to going solo yet, I will be wearing an earpiece and getting some direction.

"If you have a problem with this, we understand," she tells him. "But it was the only way we could accommodate you. We really want this opportunity to have your show be promoted on ours."

He looks at me. "And you're comfortable with this?"

I make what I hope doesn't look like a forced smile. "I think so. We've been practicing a bit and it should be okay."

He pats me on the back. "All right then. Just be sure to tell that elusive sister of yours that she owes us one."

I nod. "I'll do that."

It takes about twenty minutes before we're all set and ready to go. During this time I discover that another guest judge on the show is Eliza Wilton. I try not to act shocked, but I'm wondering what sets Eliza up as an expert. Sure, she used to do some modeling. And now she's partnering with Rhiannon. But an expert? Of course, I have to weigh that against myself. *An expert?* Ha!

"I'm a little disappointed," she tells me as we're leaving the green room. "I was really looking forward to going up against your sister today."

"*Against* her?" I frown. "You mean as in competition?"

She smiles smugly. "You obviously haven't seen this show."

She's right; I haven't—at least not an entire episode. I saw some very brief clips of it before our London trip. Not that I want Eliza to know that.

"There's always some friendly bantering and competition between the judges," she informs me. "It's part of the fun. Everyone trying to one-up everyone else."

"Right . . . fun."

She chuckles. "I'm guessing we won't have a problem with you."

"Probably not."

We go out to the set. A well-lit runway runs through the middle of the ballroom and a stage with black leather chairs and a long glass table is sitting parallel to it. Cameras and crew are positioned around the perimeter. We are introduced to the regular judges, a who's who in the British fashion world. Then we're led to our places, where we sit in front of fixed microphones—a relief, because it's one less wire to worry about.

"If you can hear me, nod." I try not to jump when I hear Dylan's voice through the earpiece. I nod as I scoot my chair a bit closer to the table.

After a few more minutes of adjustments, the lights come on and the host and former supermodel, Chloe Brinkman, does her spiel. She introduces the judges, including the guest judges, and gives a brief explanation of why I'm here in lieu of my sister. Then she gives Eliza and me a chance to say a few words about ourselves, why we are on the panel, and if anything special has caught our attention at Bahamas Fashion Week.

Eliza goes first and is almost as smooth as Paige would be if she were here. And then it's my turn, and suddenly I hear Dylan's voice in my ear. We've prearranged a cue system, so if I don't want him to speak I simply touch my chin. And that's what I do.

"I'm the co-host of *On the Runway*," I begin. "But as our viewers know, my sister, Paige Forrester, is the one who has the real fashion sense. She's a natural. In fact, she sometimes uses me as an example of fashion *don'ts*." This elicits some chuckles. "However, I've been learning a lot about fashion this year. Paige is a great teacher, even though my interests in fashion differ from hers." Then I briefly mention eco fashion, green design, and world trade.

"That's great," Chloe tells me. "You're probably aware that this has been a big focus of our show as well. You're in good company." Then she introduces the premise of their show, which is not so different from the American version, where designers compete with each other for the prize of getting to create and show their own styles at London Fashion Week next fall. "As you know we're down to the final five," she says with enthusiasm. "And they have been here in the Bahamas, working for the past two days on a resort wear outfit." She gets a catty smile. "We've made their challenge a bit more rigorous than usual, because we have limited them to only natural materials that are found on the island." She points to me. "Someone as environmentally conscious as Erin Forrester should appreciate this particular show."

Now, like any other show, the music gets loud and the spotlights turn to the runway. As the models take their turns parading up and down the platform, Dylan, who's watching them via his laptop, gives me some tips as to what is good or bad about the ensembles. And it's weird, because after the second model, I almost think I get it. Even so, I'm not sure I can verbalize it. And then, as the third model is coming out, Dylan's voice goes dead. I discreetly reach up to touch the earpiece, but it makes no difference. For whatever reason, I've lost him.

Soon it's time for critique and, although I pay attention to the other judges, I want my words to be my own. Even if I make our show look stupid, I decide to simply be myself. Design by design, I take my turn and a couple of times I even go first. I say why I think the shredded palm skirt is predictable and why the coconut husk vest is a bust. All in all, it's kind of fun. I can't believe it when the outfit I liked the most — the raffia dress trimmed in shells — wins. But I'm hugely relieved that we're finished.

"Nicely done," Mom tells me as I join my crew. "Very smooth and natural-sounding. And that comment about the coconut bust was really funny. Did Dylan come up with it?"

"As a matter of fact, Dylan and I got disconnected shortly after the show began."

She blinks. "*Really?* Well, in that case, you did a fantastic job, honey. *Good for you!*"

As we head out to the lobby, Dylan meets us. "Why didn't you use any of my comments?" he asks me in a slightly offended tone. I explain about the disconnect.

"So that was basically a waste of my time," he says in a disgruntled tone. Before I can even think of a response, Eliza joins us with her usual catty smile.

"Hey, Dylan," she says in what seems an overly familiar way. "What are *you* doing here?"

I shoot him a warning glance — I do not want him telling Eliza that I was wearing an earpiece, especially since it didn't even work.

"I just had to pick something up for my show tomorrow." He glances at his watch. "In fact, I need to get over to the Ritz to check on some things."

"Hey, that's where I'm going too. Let's share a cab." Eliza links her arm in his with a big smile. "My treat."

And just like that, they take off together. Mom doesn't even blink as she goes over her notes for the day. I'm sure she thinks it's no big deal, but I know Eliza well enough to feel a tinge of concern. Eliza has been after Dylan since the days she modeled for him in New York. And I can't help but wonder how Paige would feel if she witnessed those two trotting off together. But then I remind myself that Paige and I see things differently, and she's always telling me that I'm old-fashioned. So maybe she'd think I was making a mountain out of a molehill.

"Okay, kids," Mom says to the crew and me. "Now it's off to the Perry Ellis resort wear show. Everybody ready?"

And so goes the day, as we trek from one show to the next. In between shows, we keep checking the weather reports and the sky. This morning, it was so clear and blue that it was hard to imagine a hurricane lurking out there in the Atlantic. But as we move into the afternoon, the sky gets cloudy and has a weird greenish-yellow cast. Finally, at around four o'clock it starts to rain, hard.

Cars are lined up, waiting to pull under the protection of the hotel portico. We're running late and need to get to the next show, so we get out and make a run for it, getting soaked as we hurry inside. Thankfully, this is our last show and it's in our hotel. As we hurry through the lobby, it's obvious that people are nervous about the impending storm.

By the time we come out of the fashion show, the hurricane is bearing down on us. Crowds of people are looking out the hotel lobby windows, watching as pieces of debris and anything not tied down goes shooting by. Palm trees whip and bend in the wind, and one of them actually breaks. Both JJ and Alistair have their cameras running.

"Come away from there," Mom tells me. "It's dangerous."

The lobby is noisy and busy with people clustering about, as if unsure about what they should do. There seems to be a range of reactions and expressions—everything from party-mania to wide-eyed panic.

"We should go check on Paige and Fran," Mom says.

I invite the crew to come up with us, but they want to stay downstairs. "It's not every day you get to see a hurricane," JJ explains. "And some of these shots will be great for the show."

"I'll be watching from my room," I say. "You guys be careful."

"I asked the concierge if there were any emergency procedures we should be aware of," Mom tells me as we're waiting for the elevator. "And he just said to stay inside and away from the windows."

I laugh. "Right, I guess I won't be sitting on the terrace then."

"And, naturally, there's no way to evacuate," Mom says in a nervous tone. "Since we're on an island."

The elevator doors open and she just stands there.

"What?" I ask as I go in.

"I wonder if we should take the stairs."

"Why?"

"What if the electricity goes out?"

"Oh." I put my hand out to hold the door.

"Surely they have generators." Mom steps in and I hurry to push the button.

"Surely." I nervously watch as the floor numbers flash. "Are you scared?" I ask Mom.

She frowns. "Well, yes . . . aren't you?"

"I guess I haven't really had time to think about it."

Mom puts an arm around my shoulders, squeezing me toward her. "You know, Erin, I need to tell you how proud I am of you. The way you kept it together today. The way you're so responsible. How you've been helping Fran. Well, I know I don't tell you enough, but I am really proud of you, sweetheart."

I make an anxious laugh. "That sounds like the kind of thing someone says right before the ship sinks."

"Well, I *mean* it." Mom sighs with relief as the doors open on our floor and we both hurry out. "I'll check on Paige while you check on Fran."

When I go into Fran's room, her eyes are closed. She is so still, I actually wonder if she's breathing. But as I move closer to her bed, her eyes flutter open. "Erin," she says in a hoarse voice.

"How are you doing?" I ask as I sit in the chair beside her. She only sighs.

"The hurricane is coming."

"Yes . . . I can hear it howling out there."

"Do you want me to open the drapes so you can watch?"

She closes her eyes and I take the hint.

"How about some music?" I ask.

She doesn't react, but I go to the TV and tune it to the channel with the soothing spa music. Then I check to see if she's eaten anything from the lunch tray that I ordered from room service for her. It is untouched. Everything in me says she needs medical treatment. But with a hurricane blowing, I don't see how that's even possible.

I make some green tea and set it beside her, along with some crackers. And then, feeling helpless to do more, I go back to my room and change out of my still-damp dress and into some sweats. I look out my window to see that the storm is still raging. But from up here, it almost seems less threatening, which I'm sure is an illusion. Thanks to the hotel's generators, I'm able to turn on the TV now, tuning it to the Weather Channel. I discover I'm too restless to sit and watch, so I head to Paige's room.

"How is she?" I ask Mom when she opens the door.

"Better."

"Good."

"I got to thinking we should probably have gotten some provisions," Mom says with a worried brow.

"Provisions?"

"You know—some food and bottled water … in case we're stuck here for a while and the hotel runs out of things."

"Seriously? How long can a hurricane last?"

"Usually a few hours, but some can last up to eight or more."

"Really?"

"And it's not even solidly here yet."

"Do you want me to go forage some things from the shops downstairs?" I offer.

"It might be wise, Erin. That is, unless they've already sold out."

"Why don't you call room service and order us dinner?" I suggest. "That way we might miss the rush later."

"Good idea."

"And I'm going to do everything possible to book a flight for Fran," I say suddenly. "As soon as it's safe, I want her on a plane out of here. I don't even care how much it costs."

"That seems wise."

As I'm walking through the lobby, I try the traditional airline numbers that I saved in my iPhone this morning, but I'm getting the same results as before. The food section of the shop is picked over, but I decide to just gather up what I can, placing an odd assortment of cheese crackers, peanuts, chocolates, and some fruit drinks on the counter.

"Preparing for the storm?" The cashier grins as he begins to ring up my selection.

"Trying to. Just in case, you know."

"No worries. It will likely blow over before midnight."

"Before midnight?" I study his dark eyes. "Are you sure?"

"Oh, yeah. They never last too long. Maybe even sooner."

"Do you know how long it takes until the airlines start running again?"

"Hmm ..." He's bagging my stuff. "It depends."

I frown as I hand him a credit card.

"You're in a hurry to leave the island?"

"Yes." Then, without even meaning to, I pour out my story about how Fran needs to get out of here and back to her doctor. "I may just book an air ambulance ... but that's so expensive."

He nods with a furrowed brow. "Oh, yeah. Terribly costly." His eyes brighten. "I have an uncle with a charter airline."

"Charter airline?"

"He island hops, but he sometimes flies to the mainland too. He flies a lot of the guests in this hotel."

"Do you think he could get us to Miami?" I ask eagerly. "Tonight?"

"Maybe so." He pulls out a pad of paper, writing down a name and phone number. "You call him. Tell him Bart told you about his business."

Chapter
18

"*What?*" *my mom demands after I've spilled* my new idea for getting Fran off the island.

"I tentatively booked a charter flight out of here tonight," I say again.

"What kind of charter?"

I repeat what Bart told me about his uncle. "He uses small, fast jets. And the good news is that, thanks to the storm, he's not booked."

"*You plan to take Fran on a small charter plane and fly through a hurricane to Miami?*"

"That's not exactly how it's supposed to go." I explain how the charter service is tracking the weather and the path the hurricane is taking, and how they wouldn't do anything risky. "Their planes are valuable, Mom. It's not like they want to go up there and crash."

"I don't know, Erin."

"What are you two talking about?" Paige emerges from her bedroom looking slightly better than she did this morning. I quickly replay my evacuation plan for Fran.

Paige frowns. *"Are you nuts?"*

I glance at Mom. "Did you tell Paige what's really wrong with Fran?"

"You asked me not to mention it, Erin."

So I quickly spill out Fran's story, at least parts of it, and Paige is totally stunned. "No way," she declares. "That makes absolutely no sense. Fran's just had a bout of the flu. I heard it's been going around."

"Have you even *seen* Fran once since we arrived here?" I challenge her. "Do you know what you're talking about?"

Her brow creases. "Now that you mention it, I guess I haven't actually seen her since we got here. But she looked fine then. In fact, she looked pretty great."

"You mean because she'd lost weight?" I shake my head. "Don't you get that it's because of her leukemia? She also lost her hair—because of the chemo treatments." I realize I've probably said too much.

"The point is, Fran is very sick," Mom concurs. "She needs to get home. But I'm not sure about this plan, Erin."

"And what about this hurricane?" Paige looks worried now. "You can't fly out in weather like this."

I turn to Mom. "Please, explain it to her. I need to check with Fran and see if I can book a flight from Miami to LA tonight—otherwise it's pointless to try to get to Miami."

I head back to my room. And when I check on Fran, she's still resting quietly. I hate to disturb her. "Fran?" I whisper.

She opens her eyes, but they have an empty look now, almost as if she's given up.

"Here," I say as I help her sit up, "drink some tea." I hold the now-lukewarm cup to her lips and wait as she takes some slow sips. "You need to get your strength up a little ... so we can get you out of here and get you some medical attention."

"I don't want to go to the hospital here," she protests.

"I know. I mean Los Angeles. We're taking you home, Fran."

Her eyes brighten just a little. "Home?"

"Do you think you'll be strong enough to fly? I booked us a flight that will leave as soon as Hurricane Bruce moves safely away."

"Yes." She nods and reaches for the cup of tea. "I'll be strong enough."

"Okay. For now, just keep resting. I want you to try to eat some of your fruit from lunch. And I'll get you a yogurt from the fridge."

I get her settled then return to my room to finalize our travel plans. But first I pray, asking God to make this work. It feels like it's against all odds that we could get off the island as well as connect with a flight in Miami. I know I'm in over my head. It will take a miracle. But to my relief, the first airline I call, the one we usually use, has two first-class seats on a flight to LA. Unfortunately, that flight doesn't leave until 6:10 tomorrow morning. Even so, I book it. Then I call back the charter service and explain.

"That's probably better anyway," he assures me. "The hurricane will be well on its way by then. We'll plan to fly out of here around three in the morning, which will put us at the airport by four. That should give you enough time to check in and make your next flight. We'll call ahead for assistance. Someone can meet you at our terminal and get you to your next connection."

"Okay," I say firmly. "Book it." Then he gives me some directions, which I write down. Next, I call JJ, who's still in the lobby with the crew, and explain that Fran and I need a ride to the airport tonight.

"The airport? You can't fly out of here tonight."

Once again, I explain everything. And this time I tell him the truth about Fran. "Her condition has really deteriorated . . . she needs to get home to her doctor."

"I didn't know. Of course I'll drive you guys. No problem."

"The storm is supposed to have passed by then."

"We heard it's supposed to be on the way out by midnight."

Now I remember the crew is staying at another hotel. "You guys can use my room, if you want to weather out the storm tonight. Or maybe Paige's room, since it's bigger. She and Mom can bunk together."

"I'll tell the others."

Next I call Fran's doctor. I tell her exactly what's going on, and she sounds astounded. "Fran is in the Bahamas?" she says for the third time.

"Yes. And she's really not well." I go into some more details.

"I'm not surprised she's failing. She was insane to make that trip. I told her explicitly that it would be too much. I can't believe she didn't listen."

"She was just being optimistic," I say defensively. "She wanted to believe she was getting better."

"But it was too soon. She should've known—"

"The thing is she needs your help, Dr. Marshall. I'm trying to get her back to LA as soon as possible. We're flying out late tonight—after the hurricane passes," I say quickly before she can question that too. I glance at my notes. "We should make LA around eight in the morning. I think she'll need to see you immediately."

"I want you to get her to Cedars-Sinai Hospital. I'll call over there and get it set up." She pauses. "Are you sure she's healthy enough to make the flight?"

I honestly don't know the answer to this, but for Fran's sake, I say yes.

Hurricane Bruce is pounding down full force on the island by seven o'clock. JJ and the rest of the crew take occupancy in the suite, while Mom and Paige move into my room and I move in with Fran.

It's going to be a long night. Our room service meals finally arrive and we share them all around. With that and the provisions I snagged at the hotel store, no one goes hungry. Everyone is torn between watching the coverage on TV and looking out the window. But in Fran's room, except for the sound of the TV music, it's quiet and the drapes are drawn. I think I've done all I can to make Fran comfortable and I've packed us each one small bag. I know I'm not going to be able to sleep, so I go check on Mom and Paige.

They're in bed eating chocolate bars and watching an old Bette Davis movie. I just stand in the doorway, looking in.

"Come on in," Mom calls to me. "There's room."

So I join them and they share their chocolate with me. "How's Fran?" Paige asks.

"Resting. I think I've got what we need to travel all ready."

"And I'll pack up the rest," Mom says. We've already worked this out.

"The hotel was supposed to bring up a wheelchair—"

"Oh, yeah." Paige is looking at her iPhone now. "It came a little while ago. It's outside the door."

"So you really want to do this?" Mom asks me again.

I don't even answer. We've been over it before.

Paige shakes her phone. "I just don't get where he is."

"Who?" But even as I ask, I know.

"Dylan, of course. He's not answering. Did he say where he was going after you guys finished up *Britain's Got Style*?"

I glance at Mom and I can tell she doesn't want to answer either.

"I think he had some things to take care of for his show."

"He probably got stuck somewhere," Mom offers. "Because of the hurricane."

"What do you think the hurricane will do to the rest of Fashion Week?" I say to no one in particular. Mostly I want to change the subject. "Will they cancel shows?"

"Good question," Mom says. "I assume it will depend on the damage."

"I heard a guy on the local news saying that they get these a lot," Paige tells us. "And that in a day or two, you can't even tell the island was hit."

We chat and visit until it's so late that I can tell they're both half asleep. I return to Fran's room and sit in the chair by the window, looking out to where the wind actually seems to be slowing down some. I think perhaps Bruce is finally on his way to wreak havoc elsewhere. I've set the alarm for two, just in case I fall asleep. But my plan is to start getting us out of here a little sooner than that. In the meantime, I am praying.

I am so relieved when we are finally loaded into the first-class section of the big jet. Despite how smoothly everything else went, it was nerve-wracking and I know it has taken a toll on Fran. But, other than initially protesting the use of a wheelchair, she's been a real trouper.

"Just sleep," I tell her as I reach across and push the button to lean her chair back. "It won't be long now." I've given her half a sleeping pill. She insisted a whole one wouldn't be too much, but I'm worried. She seems so fragile. And thankfully, the half dose seems to be working.

I go over the details in my head as the jet takes off. I've already asked the flight attendant to radio to LAX so there will be wheelchair waiting at the gate. I've arranged for a town car to meet us at passenger pickup. Then it's on to the hospital. I cannot wait to feel the relief of knowing Fran is getting the care she needs.

To my surprise, I fall asleep as well. When I wake it's to the sound of the pilot announcing our arrival in LA. I am so happy I could cry, and I close my eyes and thank God.

"We're here," I tell Fran as I put her seat back into the upright position, which wakes her up. "It won't be long now."

After a slightly bumpy landing and a long taxi, we finally pull into the gate. And because we're in first class, we get to exit first. The flight attendant helps me get Fran into the wheelchair, which is right outside the plane as promised.

"Good luck," the attendant calls to us. With Fran's bag over one shoulder and my bag over the other, I wheel her through the tunnel and on toward ground transportation, where the town car is waiting. The driver helps Fran in, and we are on our way to the hospital.

By nine o'clock, Fran is checked into Cedars-Sinai Medical Center. Dr. Marshall shows up shortly afterwards to examine her.

I know I could probably leave now, but it feels weird after all we've been through to simply leave Fran here. So I sit in the waiting room and try to wrap my head around the fact that I'm no longer in the Bahamas, the hurricane is over, and I'm home in LA. I call Mom and give her an update.

"Oh, I'm so glad to hear it, Erin. You must be exhausted."

"Yeah. Pretty much. As soon as I hear how Fran is, I'll go home and shower and maybe sleep for a week."

"It's really a mess here," Mom tells me. "Power is out in places, lots of damage, beach homes destroyed, some shows are cancelled. And there's something else." She lowers her voice. "Dylan is missing."

"Missing?"

"Paige has tried and tried to call him. And she's checked his room and all around the hotel. It's like he's just vanished."

"Oh no. Do you think he was out in the storm?"

"I have no idea. Paige is frantic."

"Did you mention about him going with Eliza yesterday?" I ask carefully.

"No, no ... I don't see how that can help matters."

"No, I don't think it would either."

"I'll let you know if we hear anything about him."

"Yeah. Give Paige a hug for me. Tell her I'm praying for him."

We hang up and I do pray for Dylan. First I pray for his safety and then I pray that he doesn't break my sister's heart. Then I call Mollie, who sounds shocked to hear my voice.

"Guess what?" I say lightly.

"I don't know," she snaps back at me.

"What's wrong?"

"*What's wrong?*" She sounds seriously angry. "*What's wrong* is that I'm in labor—and it hurts!"

"*Labor?* As in having your baby?"

"It's not like I'm laboring to build a brick wall." She makes huffing noises now and I realize this girl is serious. "And if you're calling to tell me about how lovely it is in the Bahamas—I do not want to hear about it."

"Where are you?" I ask her. "I mean, are you really having the baby right now?"

"On the way to the hospital," she huffs.

"You're driving?"

"No!" More huffing. "Mom's driving."

"Which hospital?" I ask.

"Cedars-Sinai," she growls. "Like it matters. I gotta go, Erin. Have a great day!"

I cannot believe it—Mollie is on her way here, *right now*. I rush back into Fran's room, where she and the doctor are quietly discussing something. "Sorry to interrupt," I say as I start to back off.

"No, it's okay." Fran waves me over, properly introducing me to her doctor this time.

"So you're the angel," Dr. Marshall says to me.

"Not really." I wrinkle my nose. "Although I'm certain there were some real angels involved."

"Maybe so." The doctor smiles. "I was just telling Fran that I think we've found a bone marrow donor match."

"*Really?*" I look down at Fran and she has tears in her eyes.

"We need to get Fran stabilized first and get her blood counts leveled out, but we're feeling hopeful."

"Thank you so much for getting me back here," Fran tells me. "Thank you for everything, Erin."

Feeling uncomfortable with all this attention, I decide to change the subject, so I quickly tell them about Mollie being in labor. "And can you believe it—she's on her way here right now."

"*Here?*" Fran stares at me.

"I was supposed to be her birth coach, but I would've missed it if we hadn't come home last night," I tell her. "So you see what I mean—it really does feel kind of miraculous."

"You'd better go find her," Fran tells me.

"I'll check back with you later," I promise.

I'm surprised that I no longer feel sleepy as I hurry to the maternity ward to wait for Mollie. I cannot wait to see the look on her face when she sees me here. I realize that all this time I've been praying for miracles . . . and God was just waiting for the right time to deliver them.

Chapter
19

When I spot Mollie's mother pushing a wheelchair containing my best friend into the labor and delivery unit, I'm so excited that I jump up and down like a five-year-old. Mollie gapes at me as if I'm an apparition.

"Wha—what?" she gasps. "How'd you get—" She stops mid-sentence and her face gets red as she reaches down to her belly, then bends over and begins to moan.

"Erin!" Mrs. Tyson looks hugely relieved to see me. "I thought you were in the Bahamas."

"I was. It's a long story."

"Mollie started having labor pains last night, but she thought it was just indigestion. Then her water broke less than an hour ago and I think she's about to—"

"*Where is the doctor?*" Mollie cries out now.

"Can I help you?" a nurse asks.

"Yes, we called from home," Mrs. Tyson says politely. "This is Mollie Tyson and she is pre-registered and—"

"*And she's having a baby!*" Mollie screeches.

"Let's get her to a room." The nurse takes over and wheels

Mollie into a room, where she is helped to a bed and another nurse starts hooking up monitors and things.

"I'll do a quick check and we'll see how advanced you are," the first nurse tells Mollie, fitting her feet into the sock-covered stirrups.

Mrs. Tyson turns to me with a slightly horrified look. "I'm sure Mollie has told you … I'm not really good around blood and medical things."

"Why don't you sit down?" I nod to the nearby chair, but Mrs. Tyson just turns away and heads right on out the door.

So I sit in the chair. And it's weird because I don't even feel nervous. I think after all I've been through with Fran, the idea of helping Mollie have a baby isn't all that intimidating.

"Well, well, Mollie." The nurse stands up. "You're nearly eight centimeters. Did you call your doctor yet?"

"Never mind that," Mollie snaps. "If I'm that far dilated, I can have drugs, right?"

"Except that you might want to —"

"I *want* an epidural!" Mollie shouts. It's like she's someone else, but I assume it's the pain talking. And suddenly she's groaning again, tossing from side to side on the bed and yelling she needs drugs.

The nurse turns to me. "Are you her labor coach?"

I nod, looking at Mollie and wondering if this girl is even coachable. So much for her theory that it's better to have babies the natural way — I try not to recall how many times she told me she didn't want to use drugs.

"Her labor is progressing nicely and she's almost ready to go into delivery," the nurse tells me, almost like Mollie isn't here. And in some ways she's not. "It might be wise to skip the epidural and just get her into —"

Mollie interrupts her with a howl of pain. "*I want an epidural!*"

I rush over to her side and make an attempt at proper breathing, huffing and panting like a dog, trying to remember what I learned in the one birthing class I took. But it doesn't seem to matter, because Mollie's not paying attention. All she seems to want is an epidural. Before long she gets her way, and the anesthesiologist arrives with the longest needle I have ever seen.

"I'm so glad that's over with," Mollie says when the drugs begin to take effect, sounding more like her old self. "I felt like I was going to die."

"Do you want your mom to come back now?" I ask.

"Are you kidding? She wasn't even present when her own children were born."

"What?"

"She had Grant and me in prescheduled C-sections. Right here in this hospital. She's useless around anything involving blood or medical instruments."

Before long the doctor arrives and Mollie is transferred to the delivery room, where after what seems like hours, but is actually only minutes, Fern Tyson enters the world at 11:58 a.m. She is six pounds eleven ounces of pure sweetness. With fluffy dark hair and a puckered face, she is totally amazing—a real miracle. Feeling like a proud parent, I take pictures with my iPhone and send them to Mom and Paige, and, with Mollie's permission, to Blake and some of our church friends. I even send one to Tony—and that surprises me. I thought I had written Tony off months ago. But something about seeing that dark head of hair and those big dark eyes, so like her daddy's, makes me realize that Tony needs to come see his darling daughter.

While Mollie's mom and dad are in her room visiting with her, I go down to check on Fran and show her the baby pictures, which makes her smile. "What a day you've had, Erin."

"You know, I would've missed this," I tell her, "if I hadn't brought you home when I did."

"Maybe it's true what they say . . ." She sighs.

"What?"

"Maybe God does work in mysterious ways."

I nod. "I think you're right."

"Even so . . ." She looks sad. "I wish I'd had the sense not to have gone on that trip in the first place. I don't know what I was thinking. It wasn't only foolish, Erin. It was selfish."

I try to point out the positive aspects of the trip: how it was good having Mom come out, how we got some superb footage for the show, how I'm glad to be home. "Besides that, it sounds like the hurricane has really put a damper on things anyway—some of the shows were cancelled. Maybe we got out just in time, and we got what we needed while we were there." I can tell she's sleepy now, so I pat her hand, tell her to rest well, and promise that I'll come by tomorrow to visit. Then I quietly slip out.

As I'm headed back to Labor and Delivery, I'm surprised to spot Blake just coming through the entrance. Even more surprising is that Tony is with him. I greet them both then, feeling nervous about seeing Blake, I lead them over to the viewing area, proudly pointing out Fern to them. "Isn't she beautiful?"

Tony nods and I actually see tears in his eyes. "Do you think it would be okay if I go see Mollie?" he asks in a quiet voice.

I shrug. "I don't see why not. I mean, her parents might be in there. But I know Mollie would want to see you." I tell him the room number and Blake and I watch as he slowly makes his way down the corridor. Tony's dragging footsteps remind me of someone who's heading for the gas chamber.

"I got your letter," Blake tells me after we walk over to the waiting area.

"Huh?" I wonder what he means, then suddenly remember that late-night letter I wrote before the Bahamas trip. It seems so long ago. "Oh ..." I just nod. "Right."

"I think we should talk."

"Yeah, I do too," I admit. "But the truth is I'm exhausted right now, Blake. I can barely think." I tell him about the hurricane, Fran's illness, and the emergency flight ... followed by Mollie's delivery. "I'm emotionally drained."

"That's understandable." And thankfully, without questioning me further, Blake offers to take me home. I don't refuse. It's surreal as we walk through the parking garage and get into his car — like *where am I, and how did I get here?* I feel like I'm in a fog as he drives me home. But I also feel like I'm safe — like I'm in good hands — and it feels good to be with him. He even walks me all the way to my door.

"Thanks," I tell him. "You have no idea how much I appreciate this."

He smiles and I'm surprised at how much that smile comforts me. "You seem pretty beat, Erin. Get some rest and then give me a call, okay?"

"I will," I promise. And still I just stand there, staring at him.

He leans over and gives me a gentle kiss on the forehead. Nothing more ... nothing less. But as I go into the condo, I think it was perfect. It could be sheer exhaustion, but I think maybe he understands me better than I thought.

I go into the condo, drop my bag, and take a short shower followed by a nice long nap. When I wake up it's to the sound of the phone. The house phone. I pick it up to hear my sister wailing on the other end.

"Oh, Erin," she cries with too much emotion. *"You're there!"*

"Yes. I'm here. What's up?"

She makes a choked sob. "It's—it's *Dylan*."

"Oh no!" I suddenly remember how he'd gone missing during the hurricane—is it possible he was hurt? "What happened?" I ask quietly.

And then she pours out her story—and it's nothing like I was imagining (a tragic scenario where Dylan was killed beneath a collapsed building or in a car wreck). No, Paige is telling me she's just discovered that Dylan was with Eliza last night.

"You're kidding." I feel a sinking realization as I remember my concerns after we taped the *Britain's Got Style* show.

"No! He spent the night with her," she sobs. "How could he do that to me?"

"Oh, Paige. I am so sorry."

"Mom—she said that you guys saw Eliza and Dylan leave together yesterday—"

"That doesn't mean they actually slept together," I say suddenly. "I mean, you can't assume that just because they spent the night ... There was that storm and maybe they got stuck some—"

"Eliza admitted the whole thing to me," Paige says sadly. "Just a few minutes ago, down in the hotel lobby."

"Seriously?"

"Oh, she was acting all coy, like she had this big secret

and she didn't want me to figure it out. But when I asked her point blank, she laid it all out. Like she wanted to make sure I understood."

"That was just Eliza's version," I try. "Have you spoken to Dylan yet?"

"No … but I think she was telling the truth." Paige's voice is quiet and flat.

"But you don't know for sure, Paige. And you do know that girl has a mean streak. She's always been jealous of you. Maybe she's just setting you up."

"Oh, Erin, I wish you were here." Now she's crying again.

"It's going to be okay, Paige. You'll get through this. I know you will."

"I just can't believe he'd do that to me. I thought — I thought he loved me."

"I thought he did too, Paige."

"But you don't do that to someone you love."

"I don't know … I mean, I don't think so. You really need to talk to Dylan, Paige. You need to hear his side. Just in case he's innocent."

"I *know* he's not innocent." Her tone gets cold now. "In my heart, I know he did it. And I have a feeling he was just using me — right from the beginning, Erin. Remember when we were in Paris, he was worried about his future as a designer? He thought he was on his way out."

"I guess …" Now I remember how I was the one who talked to him during the paparazzi problems in London, how I encouraged him to try again with Paige. I swallow hard. Is this my fault?

"And getting engaged to me brought him fresh publicity," she continues. "It was like his ticket to another season."

"*Really?* You honestly believe that?"

"I didn't believe it then. I was too swept away. But I believe it now. Dylan knew what he was doing all along. And he used me."

"Oh ..." There's so much I want to say to her right now. But so much of it would be useless ... thoughtless ... pointless. I just don't want to go there. Besides that, I've barely recovered from all that's happened to me in the past twenty-four hours. I don't trust myself to say what I really think. And so I simply say, "I'm sorry, Paige."

"I wish I'd come home with you. I can't stand being here. And Mom just doesn't get it. She's acting like it's all going to blow over—like the aftermath of the hurricane. We'll just sweep it up and everything will be peachy keen."

"I really am sorry, Paige. I wish there was something more that I could do or say. This shouldn't have happened to you. You don't deserve this."

She sniffs. "*I trusted him.*"

"I know you did. And you can't be sorry for that."

"But it hurts so much. To give my heart like that ... and now this. What is wrong with me, Erin? Why do I attract this kind of trouble? I mean, first Ben, and now Dylan. I just want to know why!"

"I don't know why. You are an amazing person, Paige, and you deserve an equally amazing guy."

"Thanks."

"And you know that I love you, Paige. Even if Mom's acting weird right now, you know she loves you too. We're both here for you, Paige. You're not alone in this."

"I know. And that's a comfort. I just—just want to come home," she sobs.

"Why don't you? It sounds like there's not much more you can do there anyway. Why not just wrap it up?"

"Yeah . . . maybe so."

"And when you get home, we'll sit down and talk this all out. Just like sisters should."

"Yeah . . . and maybe I'll do like you, Erin—just keep the guys at arm's length for a while."

"Maybe . . . but maybe not. There's some guy stuff I want to talk to you about too, Paige."

"Really?" She sounds genuinely curious.

"Really." I sigh. "I need my sister."

She sniffs. "I need my sister too."

We express our love for each other again and as we hang up, I feel genuine grief for Paige's loss. I know she is hurting—deeply. But somehow I believe this is going to be a good thing too. She's going to learn some powerful lessons from all this pain, and eventually it will make her stronger. I also know I will be here for her. I will stand by her through her heartache, just like I hope she would stand by me. Growing up is hard to do, but I think if we don't give up and if we help each other, we can get through it. And someday we'll look back on this whole thing and just laugh. That's my hope.

DISCUSSION QUESTIONS
FOR *GLAMOUR*

1. According to Merriam Webster's dictionary, *glamour* is defined as "a magic spell; an exciting and often illusory and romantic." How does the definition impact your understanding of the title of this book?

2. Erin takes on a lot of responsibility in *Glamour* because of Fran's illness. She takes care of Fran, helps keep the show running, and keeps an enormous secret from Helen and Paige. Do you think Erin did the right thing by keeping Fran's secret? How would you have handled the situation?

3. When the two sisters hit the beach in the Bahamas, Erin refuses to take off her sarong and reveal her body. As a result Paige claims Erin isn't helping her body image cause. Erin eventually relents and unties her sarong, saying, "This is for all you girls out there who worry about not looking like a model. I don't look like one either. We need to just get over it and be thankful that we are the way we are." Would you have done what Erin did? Why or why not?

4. When Erin finds out Fran has cancer, she's understandably upset. Shauna, the girls' makeup artist, says a positive attitude is life changing, a kind of "internal makeover." When you're down, what do you do to make over your attitude?

5. Throughout the series Erin continues to have a mixed attitude toward fashion and *On the Runway*. After unintentionally missing a big fashion show Erin states, "I decide I don't really care. Let them fire me. It's not like I

ever wanted to be part of this crazy ride in the first place. Fashion is *so* not my thing. And yet I was actually enjoying it today. It figures that as soon as I'm having a good time, I make everyone else mad." What do you attribute to Erin's attitude? Do you think Erin continues to do the show solely for Paige's benefit? Or is something else pulling inside Erin?

6. After taking care of Fran and receiving very little thanks in return, Erin feels unappreciated. Have you ever been in a similar situation? What did you do?

7. Erin and Paige fight when Paige allows Dylan to spend the night in the girls' condo. Paige defends herself claiming she and Dylan are engaged and therefore it's normal and completely acceptable. Regardless of her sister's reasoning, Erin is adamantly against the idea. What do you think of the situation?

8. While Paige has no problem attaching herself to Dylan, Erin is more reluctant in relationships and continues to keep Blake at a distance. Why do you think she continually pushes Blake away though she claims to care for him?

9. The book ends with Paige thinking Dylan cheated on her. Erin suggests that Eliza is lying to Paige and that Dylan merely slept in Eliza's hotel room. Paige is still unsure. Did Erin do the right thing? How do predict the situation will be resolved in the final book?

10. Both Paige and Erin's lives have been affected by appearing on *On the Runway* — both have fame and gain some personal satisfaction from their involvement, and grow closer as sisters, but in this book they also suffer some personal losses, from Erin losing her connection to Mollie and almost missing Fern's birth to Paige getting involved with Dylan and dealing with emotional highs and lows because of him. Looking at all the girls' experiences, do you think the show as a whole has been a good thing for them?

A NOVEL

Ciao

On the Runway

Melody Carlson

Bestselling Author

Chapter
1

Los Angeles is always hot in the summertime, but when July stays in the triple digits for a week straight, I am ready to evacuate to my grandma's house in the mountains.

"You can't leave me," Mollie protests as I'm visiting her and two-week-old Baby Fern. "I'm stuck here and I would be totally lost without you."

"You guys could come with me," I say quietly as I rock the baby in my arms. Fern's almost asleep now, sucking on her pacifier, eyelashes fluttering on her cheeks.

Mollie chuckles. "Yeah, right. You've told me how your grandmother lives—it's like going back in time. No, thank you. Besides, what about your grandma's new boyfriend? She might not want any company with him around."

"That's possible." I lean over the side of Fern's crib, trying not to disturb her as I gently lay her down, adjusting her pacifier and tucking the baby blanket around her. Fortunately, Mollie's basement apartment stays nice and cool despite this heat wave.

Satisfied that Fern is down for the count, we go to the other side of the room where we open some sodas and I pop my *Britain's Got Style* disc into her DVD player. The episode already aired in England, but it won't be on our show until early August. "Like I told you, Paige was supposed to be a judge," I explain as Mollie turns on the TV.

"But she was nursing a hangover," Mollie fills in.

"Right. Anyway, I was wearing an earpiece, and Dylan was supposed to be feeding me fashion critique."

"Seriously?" She frowns at me.

"Yeah, it sounds lame now, but at the time it made sense."

"So what's going on with that jerk anyway?" She pauses the DVD. "Give me the dirt on Dylan."

I groan and lean back in the chair, trying to remember the latest development in the ongoing drama of Paige Forrester and Dylan Marceau's engagement. "Well, I already told you that he's been sending her flowers and chocolates and shoes—"

"*Shoes?*" Mollie's expression is a combination of outrage and lust.

"Oh, you know, nothing says 'I'm sorry' like a pair of Louboutins."

"Yeah, that red sole is like a big ol' bleeding heart." She takes a sip of soda and rolls her eyes. "So what's Paige's response?"

I shrug. "She finally had an actual conversation with him a couple days ago."

"*And?*" Mollie leans forward with way too much interest. But I have to forgive her. It's not easy being cooped up with a newborn 24/7.

"I think she's kind of torn. I mean, on the one hand, it's hard *not* to believe Dylan. I honestly thought he was in love with Paige too. And it's possible that Eliza set him up while we were in the Bahamas. We know she's capable of something like that."

"Maybe so, but wasn't it *his* choice to share a room with her?"

I nod. "Paige specifically asked him why he didn't just camp out in the lobby until the hurricane moved on."

Mollie nods. "And he said?"

"He said he didn't think it was that big a deal and that he didn't mean to fall asleep on the sofa, but it was late. And he said that Paige should just trust him."

Mollie laughs. "Trust him? Overnight in a hotel room with a beautiful woman? And let's not forget, she's a beautiful *rich* woman."

"That's true." I recall Eliza's interest in remaining in the fashion world even though her modeling career fizzled. To be honest, this is one facet of the dilemma I hadn't fully considered before. But if Dylan's design firm really is struggling, as Paige has suggested, it's possible that linking himself to an heiress would be a tempting bailout plan.

"And you said that Eliza has had her eye on Dylan for a while, right?"

"Eliza was totally into Dylan during New York Fashion Week, and even more so when we stayed at her parents' chateau in France. And you should've seen Eliza in the Bahamas when she congratulated Paige on her engagement. She was pea green with envy."

"So ... what if it really was a setup?" Mollie asks in an intrigued tone. "What if Eliza planned the whole thing right from the start—a way to trap Dylan and hurt Paige?"

"I don't know. It seems a little far-fetched."

"But what if Eliza, knowing the hurricane was coming, talked Dylan into taking her to that other hotel where she already had the suite booked? Maybe she pretended she needed his help, somehow enticed him up to her room ... and then slipped him a mickey." Mollie looks at me with wide eyes. "What do you think?"

I laugh. "I *think* you've been watching too many old Hitchcock movies."

"It could've happened. Then after it was all said and done, Eliza acted like they'd had a little tryst and—"

"But why wouldn't Dylan just say that?" I shake my head. "No, I think Paige is right. Maybe Dylan's been using her all along."

"You think he's used her to promote his clothing line?" Mollie purses her lips like she's ruminating over this. "Yeah, I guess that's believable. Paige Forrester *is* a hot commodity in the fashion world. A designer could do worse than engage himself to someone like her—even if it's just for a short spell."

"I really hate to think of Dylan like that."

"But he's a businessman, Erin. He has employees, and the bottom line. He might've rationalized that he was simply saving his ship."

"But how does he look now? I mean, if word gets out that he was just using Paige?" I ask her.

She frowns. "Good point. But maybe that's why he has to move on to another girl—one with a lot of money."

"I don't know, Mollie. That just makes it all so sad and pathetic, especially for Paige. It's like she was blindsided."

"Life's like that sometimes."

"I just didn't think Dylan was that kind of a guy."

Mollie sets down her soda with a clunk. "Guys are so flaky."

I'm tempted to point out that not all guys are like that. But I realize that will only start an argument and will also initiate Mollie's questions about my personal life. So far I haven't told her much about what's going on between Blake and me. In fact, I haven't told anyone—perhaps because I'm still trying to wrap my head around it myself. Am I really ready to be as serious as Blake seems to want? Do I want to take it to the next level?

"Speaking of flakes . . ." I smirk at her. "How's old Tony boy?"

Mollie rolls her eyes.

"Blake tells me that Tony's been coming to visit you."

She tips her head toward the crib. "More like to visit his daughter."

"But that's kind of cool, isn't it?"

She makes a lopsided smile. "I guess."

"And when he comes to visit Fern, I suppose the two of you don't talk at all?"

She shrugs. "We talk, a little."

"So . . . what have you been talking about?"

"I don't know." She shrugs and doesn't meet my eyes.

"Fine. Just keep on being tightlipped about the whole thing. All you'll do is make me even more curious." I point my finger at her. "In fact, now I'm suspicious. I'll bet you two are getting back together, aren't you?"

She scowls at me. "No way."

"No way on your end, or no way on Tony's?"

"No way—on my end."

I blink. "Seriously?" I find this hard to believe, especially considering how she's been pining away for her ex for months.

She nods. "I told Tony that even if he begged me—if he got down on his hands and knees and crawled over broken glass—I would still not go back to him."

"And what was his reaction to that?"

Her mouth twists to one side. "Probably relief."

"So does that mean he was *asking* you to go back to him?"

"Not exactly. He was more what-iffing. Like *what if* we got back together? *What if* we became a little family? Would it work?"

"Would it?"

Mollie's expression softens a bit. "Sometimes I wonder if it would."

"And?"

She laughs. "And then I wake up and realize I was just dreaming."

I actually feel relieved at this. Not that I wouldn't want Mollie to get back with Tony—if it's the right thing. But I've seen her hurt so badly, wounded so deeply . . . I wouldn't want her to jump back into it again. "Well, anyway, I think it's cool that Tony is interested in seeing his daughter."

Mollie brightens. "And he's promised to pay child support too."

"Good for him."

She nods. "Yeah. But that means he can't move out of his parents' place like he'd been planning. And he'll have to keep working once school starts in the fall—just part-time, but he'll be pretty tied down."

"Not as tied down as you."

"That's true. But at least I'll be going back to school too. More than ever, I want to finish my degree now. I have to."

I want to ask her about acting, but hate to make her feel bad. I know becoming an actress had been her dream, but I also know that aspiration got set on the back burner during her pregnancy. Maybe it's dead and buried now.

"So what's going on with the show these days?" Mollie asks.

"Mostly we've been putting together the Bahamas shows," I tell her. "I'm still getting to intern in the editing room."

"Cool."

"Yeah, it's a great way to learn."

"So when does your show go on hiatus?"

"All of August. After that we'll get ready for Italy. Early September is Milan Fashion Week. It's supposed to be really good, and most of the top designers in the world will—"

Mollie holds up her hand. "Sorry I asked. That's all I need, you know, when I'm scrambling around here, changing stinky diapers and trying to keep up with my homework. It'll just totally make my day to imagine you and Paige roaming around Italy."

"Hey, if it turns out anything like the Bahamas trip, I'd rather be in your shoes, going to classes and taking care of Fern."

"Yeah, right. I'm sure there'll be a hurricane in Italy, Erin." Her voice drips with sarcasm. "No, you and Paige will be hob-nobbing and shoe shopping and I'll be stuck here doing the laundry. Do you have any idea how many loads of laundry I do a week?"

I shrug.

She makes a dramatic groan. "You and Paige … man, you guys have the life."

I wish I hadn't mentioned Milan to her. Sometimes I forget that Mollie still has some serious jealousy issues. "So maybe we shouldn't watch this DVD either."

"No, no, I want to see that. I have a feeling it'll be pretty funny."

"You mean that *I'll* be pretty funny?"

She grins as she aims her remote at the TV. "Hey, you've never claimed to be a fashion expert, Erin. So shoot me for wanting to see you floundering on an international TV show. I'm only human."

But as we watch *Britain's Got Style*, I can tell that Mollie is a bit disappointed. Not only do I not totally flounder, I get more camera time than Eliza. Plus I get some laughs—not all at my expense either.

"Who knew?" Mollie says once the show is over.

"Who knew what?"

"That Erin Forrester is finally starting to get fashion."

I glance at my watch. "And now Erin Forrester needs to get going." As I gather my stuff, I explain that I promised to visit our producer, Fran, this evening and leave the DVD with her.

"How's she doing?" Mollie asks with concern.

"She's scheduled next Tuesday for her bone marrow transplant. She just needs to remain stabilized until then."

"Oh, good. I'll keep praying for her."

"She'll appreciate that." I hug Mollie and tell her good-bye then head outside. Despite the fact it's close to eight o'clock, the temperature still feels like it's in the high nineties.

Fran's out of the hospital and back in her apartment now. Her mom even flew in from Boston to stay with her awhile. She's only been here a few days, but it's obvious they don't get along too well, which is why I've been trying to drop in sometimes, just to lighten the otherwise heavy atmosphere. After all I've been through with Fran during her cancer treatments, I can't just turn away. Maybe it's my calling to help others. Whether it's Mollie, Fran, or Paige, it seems that I've been doing a lot of hand-holding lately. But I'm okay with it — I think it's what Jesus would do.

Chapter
2

I'm barely in the door at Fran's apartment when I realize that Mrs. Bishop is on some kind of tirade. As she lets me in, her cheeks are flushed and she's all worked up about something. "Come in, come in," she says in an aggravated tone.

"Mother's been trying to convince me to go home with her," Fran tells me from the sofa. She's wearing a forced smile and her eyes look tired.

"Only because it makes perfect sense." Mrs. Bishop is pacing back and forth between the tiny dining area and the living room. "I could care for you in the convenience of my own home and—"

"It would be convenient for you, Mother. Not for me." Fran is pushing herself to her feet, and I can tell she's struggling. I rush over to help, giving her my arm to pull herself up.

"We have excellent doctors and medical facilities in Boston." Mrs. Bishop stops walking, staring at us as I'm guiding Fran toward her room.

"I think Fran might need to go to bed," I say.

"Yes. Fine." Mrs. Bishop waves her hand in the way a queen might dismiss a servant. Then she follows as I slowly walk Fran down the short hallway. "But I want you to listen to me, Fran. There is nothing you have here in Los Angeles, well except for this stinking heat, that we don't have in Boston."

"Boston can get hot—"

"It's not hot now. I just spoke to your father and he says it's in the midseventies and there's a nice breeze—"

"Yes, Mother, and I'm glad the weather is nice there. But the point is, my doctors are *here*. And I'm scheduled to—"

"We have the finest doctors in the world in Boston, Francis Marie, and you know it."

We've arrive in Fran's bedroom, and I'm hoping that Mrs. Bishop will back off, but she doesn't. Whether it's the LA heat or her Bostonian stubbornness, this woman is relentless tonight. Finally, with Fran sitting breathlessly on the edge of her bed, I turn to Mrs. Bishop. "I know you love your daughter, but right now Fran needs some rest. So maybe you could have this conversation with her another time—when she's stronger."

Mrs. Bishop's brows arch, but fortunately she takes the hint and leaves the room. "Sorry," I say to Fran as I help her lie down, "I didn't mean to sound so bossy, but—"

"Bossy?" Fran lets out a weary chuckle as she leans back. "Who are you kidding? My mom wrote the book on bossy."

"Well, I just thought you needed a break."

She closes her eyes and sighs. "I did. Thanks."

"Can I get you anything?"

"Just some water and my pills over there on the dresser."

"How about something to go along with the pill?" I ask as she puts one in her mouth. I know how irritated her stomach has been since starting chemo again. "A little toast and yogurt maybe?"

She shrugs then washes the pill down with a sip of water.

"I'll take that as a yes," I say as she sets the water glass on her bedside stand. Then I return to the living room, where Mrs. Bishop has resumed her pacing. This woman reminds me of a bird. Not a dainty sort of bird — more like a chicken, with her rounded body and thin legs. And the jerky way she moves about, almost as if she's pecking, is kind of hen-like too.

"I'm getting Fran a snack," I tell her.

"She already had dinner."

"Great." I nod. "But it's good for her stomach to have a little food with her medicine."

"I suppose."

As I wait for the bread to turn to toast, I attempt to talk some sense into Mrs. Bishop. "You know, Fran is comfortable here in her apartment ... and with her doctors and Cedars-Sinai, and I don't think it would be in her best interest to move her just now."

"How old are you?" Mrs. Bishop demands out of the blue.

I blink. "Nineteen."

She laughs. "You're nineteen, with a role in a kids' reality show? What makes you think you're an expert on how to make my daughter well?"

Just then the toast pops up, and I distract myself by applying a very thin layer of butter, the way Fran likes it. I cut it into fourths and set it on a small plate. Then with the yogurt in one hand and the toast in the other, I face this outspoken woman. "It's true, I'm young. And I'm not an expert," I say evenly. "But I really do care about your daughter."

"Humph." She gives me a skeptical look. "I'm guessing you care more about your job and that Fran is your meal ticket than you do —"

"*Excuse* me." I lock eyes with her, ready to hurl some facts at her. But instead I walk away. I take Fran's snack into her room, closing the door a little too loudly behind me.

"Let me guess," Fran says in a weary voice. "Mother is setting her sights on you now."

I shrug. "It's okay."

"Sorry."

"Just eat what you can," I say as I arrange the food on the tray and set it on her bed. I sit down and give her the update on Paige and Dylan. Naturally, I pad the story, making it seem more pleasant and hopeful than it really is. I suspect Fran knows there's more to it, but I decide perhaps this is a game we both have agreed to play ... the Pollyanna game. At least until she's better. I just hope that she *will* get better. I'm praying (and asking everyone else to pray too) that the transplant will work and turn things around for her. Because I have a feeling if things don't turn around, Fran won't last too long. I just wish Fran's mom got this.

When I'm sure that Fran's asleep I tiptoe out and find, to my relief, that Mrs. Bishop is not around. I suspect by the sound of the television that she's retired to the guest room for the evening. I let myself out, locking the door behind me. Then as I'm walking to my car I hit speed dial, finally returning Blake's call from earlier this evening.

"Hey, Erin." Blake's tone is warm and friendly.

I tell him where I am and what I've been doing, and he invites me to meet him for coffee on my way home. "Maybe an iced coffee," I say as I get into my Jeep.

"Great. I have something I want to talk to you about."

I tell him I'll be there in fifteen minutes. As I'm driving, I get curious. What is it that he wants to talk to me about? It's not like we don't talk a lot these days. In fact, since I got home from the Bahamas, we've been in closer contact than ever. I realize it's partly the result of the letter I wrote him, apologizing and confessing that I have some fears and inhibitions when it comes to relationships. It's like when I opened up to him, it opened a new door in our friendship. And now he wants to specifically talk about something.

It seems only natural to suppose that he wants to talk about *us*. Before I broke it off with him, he'd wanted to elevate our relationship to the next level. I'm curious if that's what he wants now. In some ways, I think I'd be open to committing to an exclusive relationship with him now. In fact, that might actually simplify life a bit. Like I'd know he was there for me, and I'd be there for him. No more playing games and guessing. Really, I'm thinking as I pull into a parking spot near Starbucks, that might be pretty cool.

"Hey, there you are!" Blake hugs me, kissing me on the cheek.

"How was work?" I ask as we go inside and get in line. Blake's been working this summer for an uncle with a landscaping business.

"Hot and grueling," he admits.

"But look at that tan," I say as I touch his cheek. "Hopefully you're using sunscreen."

He nods. "Yeah, my mom's been all over me about that."

We order our iced mochas then go sit down. Blake is grinning like he's got a sweet secret and I'm dying of curiosity, but I don't want to be pushy. Instead, I tell him about Fran's pushy mother. "She actually thought I was being nice to Fran just to secure my job. She said Fran was my meal ticket. Can you believe that?"

He laughs. "That just shows how out of touch the poor woman is."

"I guess." I smile at him. I'm not sure if it's just me or his tan or the fact that his hair is longer than usual, but it seems like Blake gets more handsome each day. I'm about to mention this when our mochas are ready and Blake goes to get them.

As he's walking back, I decide that if he is about to ask me to be in an exclusive relationship with him, I will definitely, absolutely, say yes!

"Here you go, my lady." He sets my drink in front of me and sits down.

I take a sip. "Mmm ... delish. Thanks!"

"And I'll bet you're wondering why I asked you here tonight."

"Yeah." I give him a hopeful smile and wait.

"Well, Ben called me this afternoon."

I blink. "Ben? Benjamin Kross?"

He smiles. "Yeah. Who else?"

I shrug and try not to show my disappointment, which is twofold. One part is that I suspect this conversation is not going to be about our relationship after all, and another part is that I really wish Blake and Ben would part ways. It was sweet that Blake befriended Ben at first—back when Paige and Ben were dating, and when Ben needed a friend after Mia Renwick, Ben's reality show co-star, died. But when I saw him in France, it seemed that Ben was intent on returning to his selfish, shallow ways, and I can't imagine how Blake has any positive influence on him.

"Anyway ..." Blake smiles broadly. "Ben's in on the ground floor of a new reality show."

"A new reality show ... just what this world needs," I say in a cynical tone that I instantly regret.

His smile fades. "So, it's okay for you and Paige to have a reality show, but no one else?"

"Sorry. That was just my exhaustion showing." I force a smile.

"Okay." He nods. "So anyway, Ben and his producer have been pitching this new show and it sounds like this one network is really interested, and—guess what?"

"I have no idea."

"Ben's invited me to be part of it." Blake is beaming now. "Can you believe that?"

I'm trying to wrap my head around all this. Ben wants Blake to be part of his reality show? "Seriously?"

"Yeah. It would be so cool, Erin. For starters, I could quit working for my uncle—talk about slave labor. Do you know how miserable it is to do yard work in this heat? Plus, I'll be able to make enough money to go to film school. I mean, later on, after the TV show ends."

I nod. I know how unhappy Blake's been with his dad's pressure to get a "real" degree. And how disappointing his first year of college was. Going to film school was Blake's dream even before it became mine. It seems that both our dreams got put on hold last year.

"Wow." I try to make a genuine-looking smile. "That's cool, Blake. Tell me about the show." It takes all my self-control not to rain on this parade, or jump to negative conclusions, or to point out that party-boy Benjamin Kross's show will probably end up a train wreck.

"It's called *Celebrity Blind Date*."

"*Celebrity Blind Date?*"

"Yeah. There'll be an ongoing cast of guys and girls who are semi-known, you know, kinda celebrities—like B-listers." He chuckles. "Actually they're more like C- or D-listers. And with the aid of a computer dating service, which will be one of the show's sponsors, they'll go on blind dates."

"Real blind dates?"

"Well, as real as anything can be in reality TV. Naturally, the cameras will be around, but Ben wants them to be sort of incognito. And at the beginning and ending of each episode the daters—"

"The daters?"

"You know, the regular cast—the pseudocelebs. Anyway, they'll gather somewhere, like a restaurant or club, and they'll discuss the dates—like what went wrong or right or whatever."

"It actually sounds like an interesting premise."

"It is!" His face lights up.

"And so did you tell Ben you would do this—for sure?" I'm hoping there's still a chance for Blake to escape the crazy world of reality TV.

"I told him I wanted to think about it."

"And what *do* you think?" It's a silly question, because I can tell by his expression that he's already on board.

"It's a huge opportunity, Erin. I think I want a piece of the action." He gets a thoughtful look. "But I'm curious ... what do *you* think about it?"

"Really?"

"Sure, you're my best friend, Erin. I want your opinion."

"Well ..." I pause to consider my words. I don't want to ruin this for him. "You know how a reality show can mess with your life, Blake. You've seen the kinds of trials Paige and I have gone through. And that being in the spotlight comes with a price."

"I know." He nods. "I've had a front row seat, Erin. I'm well aware of the downside of the business. I'd be going in with my eyes wide open."

"Well, at least as wide open as possible," I caution. "But you never know what's around the next corner, Blake. I mean, even this thing with Paige and Dylan—it's really a by-product of our show."

"Are you saying Paige wouldn't have gotten her heart broken if you guys weren't doing the show?" He studies me closely.

"Hmm ... good point."

"Life is life, Erin. Whether it's on film or on the streets, it happens. And this blind date show—well, I'll admit it's not going to save the planet, but I still think it'll be good fun. And it will look great on my résumé for film school."

"That's what I keep hearing."

"So anyway. I think I'll call Ben and tell him to count me in."

"What will your dad say about this?"

Blake frowns. "Oh, you know, he'll give me his free lecture about the real world and how I need a real job—but I'm sure he'll back off once he sees my mind is set."

Seeing his mind *is* set, I decide not to point out any more potential pitfalls to his plan. "So when do you think it'll go into production?"

"Assuming the network gives him the thumbs-up, Ben said he wants to get it rolling as soon as possible. He's worried that someone else might try to snatch his idea."

"I'm curious, Blake. How do you see your faith playing into the whole thing?"

"My faith is part of who I am, Erin. And Ben actually appreciates that too. He said he wants me to be up front with it. It'll provide some interesting contrast within the show."

"Like you'll be the angelic boy amidst all the little devils?"

He chuckles. "Maybe not quite like that. But Ben wants to have a diverse cast."

"Meaning it won't just be a bunch of the old *Malibu Beach* kids—the ones who've outgrown that show?"

"He'll probably use a few of them. But he'll hire some new faces too."

Suddenly I feel very tired. "You know, it's been a long day," I tell him. "I should probably get going. And I need to check on Paige. She's still pretty fragile."

"When is she going public with the breakup?" Blake asks as he walks me to my Jeep.

"I'm not sure." I glance at him. "You didn't tell Ben, did you?"

"No. I promised you I wouldn't. You can trust me."

"Good." I sigh as I unlock my vehicle. "To be honest, I'm not totally sure they *are* breaking up."

"Are you kidding? After what Dylan pulled?"

I shake my finger under his nose. "Remember . . . innocent until proven guilty."

"Right." He leans down and kisses me on the cheek. "Be safe."

As I drive home, I'm mulling over two things. First and foremost is Blake's big news. And while I know this is a good career break for him and I should be happy, an unsettling cloak of worry wraps itself around me. What if this "opportunity" derails Blake? What if it unravels him the way I've seen it unravel so many others? The other thought nagging me right now is that brotherly peck Blake gave me as a goodnight kiss. What did that mean anyway? That his interest toward me has suddenly cooled now that he's got a hot new project to leap into? And, if that's the case, how does that make me feel?

On my way up the stairs to the condo, I remember my hopeful expectation as I drove to Starbucks. I was actually getting ready to tell Blake, "Yes! I want to be in an exclusive relationship with you!" Now, instead of taking that next step, I'm trying to accept that my would-be boyfriend might be participating in a reality show about dating—*dating other girls!*

Premiere

Melody Carlson

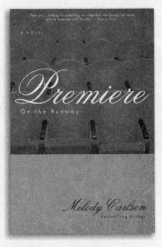

A recipe for success or a design for disaster?

Although they're sisters, Paige and Erin Forrester are like oil and water, night and day, denim and silk. Paige is an out-going fashionista who loves to be the center of attention, while Erin is more comfortable sporting vintage garb and recording the action around her. When a near disaster turns into the opportunity of a lifetime, these two very-different sisters are given the chance to star in their own fashion-TV show. A guest spot on a hot teen-reality series and their first big red-carpet assignment give this unlikely partnership plenty of room for success—and even more for failure.

Available in stores and online!

Catwalk

Melody Carlson

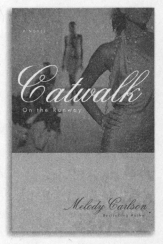

Big Apple. Bigger Problems.

The success of the Forrester sisters'
On the Runway TV show lands them
a hot ticket to Fashion Week in New
York City. Paige is determined to gar-
ner the attention of New York's top
designers, but her newfound fame
threatens to go to her head. Erin wants
to help promote the work of some eco-minded designers, but
struggles to be taken seriously. Can Paige keep her prima donna
behavior in check? Will Erin's involvement hurt the people she's
really trying to help? Success in the big city comes with even bigger challenges, and as the pressure grows, so does the drama.

Available in stores and online!

Rendezvous

Melody Carlson

Lost in translation?

Having learned some hard lessons about the costs of recklessness and fame, sisters Paige and Erin Forrester feel ready to take their fashion-focused TV show on location to Paris. Unfortunately, it doesn't take long for many of their good intentions to get lost in translation. An unplanned week of filming at runway model Eliza Wilton's family estate leads to romance, jealousy, and surprises. With cameras rolling, both girls have to be careful or the future of *On the Runway* could end up as wobbly as Paige's stiletto heels.

Available in stores and online!

Spotlight

Melody Carlson

Feeling the heat.

On the Runway has become a global phenomenon, and when Paige and Erin Forrester take their reality show to London, they get a reception to remember. Bombarded by crazed fans and the flashbulbs and interrogations of the infamous British paparazzi, the sisters know that their lives have changed—big time. Star treatment has its perks, but the girls quickly learn just how scorching life in the limelight can be. Before long, the sisters are stretched close to a breaking point. With zealous paparazzi poised to take advantage of even the slightest whiff of a scandal, the stakes have never been higher.

Available in stores and online!

On the Runway Series

Ciao

Melody Carlson

The sweet life might just turn sour.

After the events in the Bahamas, Paige's engagement to designer Dylan Marceau is about to fall apart—and so is Paige. Erin's state of mind isn't much better. In addition to keeping Paige in check, Erin is dealing with Bryce's new TV career, as well as having to care for Fran during her chemo. A trip to Milan might be the break both girls need, but things only seem to get more complicated once they land in Italy. Dylan is also in Milan, and Paige's rekindled romance, combined with a new director, leaves Erin with more work on the show. Just when Erin can't take any more, she discovers a secret that could crush Paige. Clinging to God for direction, Erin must find the power to make a difficult choice, one that could not only hurt her sister but throw the show into turmoil.

Available in stores and online!

Carter House Girls Series
from Melody Carlson

Mix six teenage girls and one '60s fashion icon (retired, of course) in an old Victorian-era boarding home. Add boys and dating, a little high-school angst, and throw in a Kate Spade bag or two ... and you've got the Carter House Girls, Melody Carlson's chick lit series for young adults!

Mixed Bags
Book One

Stealing Bradford
Book Two

Homecoming Queen
Book Three

Viva Vermont!
Book Four

Lost in Las Vegas
Book Five

New York Debut
Book Six

Spring Breakdown
Book Seven

Last Dance
Book Eight

Available in stores and online!

Talk It Up!

Want free books?
First looks at the best new fiction?
Awesome exclusive merchandise?

We want to hear from you!

Give us your opinions on titles, covers, and stories.
Join the Z Street Team.

Email us at zstreetteam@zondervan.com
to sign up today!

Also—Friend us on Facebook!

www.facebook.com/goodteenreads

- Video Trailers
- Connect with your favorite authors
- Sneak peeks at new releases
- Giveaways
- Fun discussions
- And much more!